The

Thrilling

Chronicles

of Mayfield

Aubrey Lewis

Illustration By Marcus Bettis

Dedication

This book is dedicated to my daughter Tori Lewis, my friends and everyone who has memorable moments in Middle School. These are the times in our lives where friendship is made and character evolves within us.

Acknowledgments

I thank my Mother's Treshunda Aubrey and Latrecia McCoy for encouraging me to continue writing, even in the midst of adversities. My father Gary Aubrey for always supporting me. My grandmother Eliza Tate for her wisdom and most importantly my husband, Terrocus Lewis for loving me unconditionally. A special thanks to my editor at BLIPUBLISHING, Ivy McQuain for seeing potential within me and taking me under her wings.

Table of Content

Chapter 1:   A Family No More

After two years of back and forth marriage counseling, my mom and dad decided to throw in the towel. I knew it would eventually happen because my dad, for some reason, started sleeping on the couch.   Or when I woke up early in the morning, I found my dad asleep in the guest room, instead of in bed with my mom. I always wondered, 'how can two people love each other, but yet hate each other at the same time?'

When I asked my mom that, all she would say is, "Sarah, just keep on living."

That was her way of telling me to mind my own business and stay out of adult's business so I knew not to continue asking, although I really don't know what she meant.

If I had to look forward to screaming and yelling all day long, then I didn't want to look forward to getting married. When my parents divorced, my mom decided to move back to her hometown, to be closer to my grandma and as far away from my dad as the road would take her.

If I wasn't in school when they started the divorce then my mom would have left my dad sooner. But it was the summer and there was nothing stopping her, not even the thought of our broken family.

It's early in the morning and my mom has me loading the car. With each box I put in the car sadness is capturing my soul. I don't want to leave my daddy behind and I certainly don't want to leave my friends either. Just the idea of having to start middle school as a new student keeps me from being excited about this forced new chapter in my life.

I am literally terrified at the idea of having to make new friends and get familiar with a different lifestyle. To make matters even worse my parents are not even speaking to each other. It's just silence as we pack the car.

Box after box, the two were silent. "Are you sure you don't want to take anything else," my dad asks.

"Nothing that the two of us bought together," my mom says.

She knows that the family house in which we are going to is fully furnished. Whenever we go visit my grandma in Arkansas, we stay in the family house that she bought when she received a large lump sum of money after my grandpa passed away.

This must be the hardest experience of my life... leaving all of my friends. I throw my last box of all my things in the car and run to meet them at the corner where they are all standing looking as sad as I am feeling. I don't want to say goodbye but I have to.

"Do you have to leave Sarah?" one of my friends asks, with tears in his eyes. "Whose house are we going to play basketball at, or eat snow cones, or even jump on the trampoline at? No one likes us in their yards, so we'll have to find somewhere else to play."

Wiping away my tears, I say, "You can still shoot in my basketball goal. I'll make sure that my dad lets you play, okay? I promise I'll be back soon. Now group hug."

"Come on Sarah, time to go sweetie," my mom says as she pulls away from my dad's hug.

Saying goodbye, my dad kisses my forehead gently and reaches into his pocket. He pulls out his pocket watch that my grandfather gave him (he carries this watch around everywhere).

"Keep this with you Sarah, and know that as long as this watch ticks, so will my love for you."

"Love you too daddy," I say as I get in the car and he closes the door behind me.

As we begin to cross the Golden Gate Bridge, leaving San Francisco quickly becomes a reality.   Unbuckling my seatbelt, I turn around, and stare out at the beautiful skyline for one last time.   The skyline buildings so tall, they rank the second tallest buildings on the pacific coast region... I smirk 'cause I learned this in school and felt proud of my city.

"There's no way the buildings in Arkansas will be as beautiful as San Francisco's skyline," I mumble under my breath as I watch San

Francisco get smaller and smaller. Eventually, everything becomes a blur, partially because of the tears in my eyes and partially because of the cloud cover. I stare until I can't see the 555 California Street Building formerly known as Bank of America Center or the 345 California Center Parking Garage. I eventually close my eyes and cry to myself so my mom wouldn't feel horrible for ripping me away from my dad and my friends.

After two days of traveling, we finally made it to our new home. Before I could even think about unloading the car, I quickly run into the house to call my friend Cynthia, who I met when I came to Arkansas a few visits ago.   She lives in the same neighborhood, just a block away.   Excited about my arrival she hangs up the phone and hop on her bike to come over.   I couldn't wait to see her, so I run to the corner of our four way street and wait for her.

'Arkansas is so different from San Francisco,' I think to myself as I look at all the trees.   As I am waiting for Cynthia, I listen to birds chirping and I know I'm definitely in the country.   I'm still not happy that we moved, but I'm happy we are in a place where I have at least one friend.   One friend was better than starting a new school with no friends at all.

Chapter 2: Starting Something New

At last, seventh grade is finally here. I thought I would never make it through sixth grade, especially with those immature sixth grade boys. I don't know how my friends and I learned especially with them always wanting to cheat off of our tests and ask us if we would do their homework for candy and extra lunch. I mean I don't mind helping from time to time but every test and all of the answers?

I remember this one boy, Josh Harmon, who would flirt with all the girls in my class, as if he didn't know that we thought he was absolutely disgusting. Ugh! Ack! Gross!

He would literally drop anything on the floor, just to bend down and look under the girls' skirts. I thought it was disgusting, so I convinced my mom not to buy me any skirts the entire school year. Some of the girls that thought he's cute took it to their advantage to flirt back, just so he would walk them to their locker, ask them to sit next to them at lunch or wait by their locker like a lost puppy. I didn't take part in getting his attention, but I most certainly took part in getting extra lunch when he offered.

It's the first day of seventh grade and at my new school and I realize that playing along with Josh may have done more harm than good. I really didn't study hard and now I'm scared that math may be like a foreign language to me. I know that if I want to make a passing grade in math class that I have to apply myself much harder.

'Oh great, just what I need... the fear of failing a class at a new school with only one friend,' I thought to myself as I walked down the hall towards my first period class.

"This is going to be a long day," I mumbled under my breath as I pass everyone staring at me as if I were a wild animal. I clearly have new girl scent on me.

As the bell rings I watch everyone focus on hustling to their first period classes. I have no desire to hurry and soon my stomach starts to turn in knots. I always get nervous before I do something new. I start to slow down because I know that once I enter into the class that everyone is going to stare at me and someone will more than likely even try to be mean to me. It happens to all the new kids. I watched it happen in San Francisco all the time.

The bell rings and it scares me that I jump while walking in and everyone erupts in laughter. I just put my head down and walk towards the teacher. She's a pretty lady, tall and skinny with beautiful brown skin. She gently places her hand on my shoulder and I look up to see Cynthia wildly waving her hand as if she is trying to land a plane. I smile at her while avoiding the eye contact of everyone else. It was different an all-Black school in all different shades. I was use to kids of all colors so I was frightened, but excited to see so many Blacks in one classroom.

She clears her throat and immediate everyone got quiet. "Everyone this is Sarah Taylor. Let's welcome her to class," Mrs. Jones said with a southern accent that I only hear when I come to visit my family here in Arkansas so I chuckle to myself.

"Hi," everyone says in unison and then one voice shouts out, "Mrs. Jones, where she from?"

"Where is she from," she immediately corrects the loud boy and then she turns to me and holds out her hand and tilts her head for me to respond.

I want to faint because I don't know

anyone but Cynthia and standing in front of everyone to tell my name and where I am from is slow death.   Before I say where I am from I hear Cynthia say California and I look up to see her smiling.

"Shut up Cynthia, you don't know her," the boy says with a scowl on his face.

I immediately jump to Cynthia's defense, "I am from California and she does know me, she's my friend." All the students say "ooooo" and then erupt in laughter.   Mrs. Jones looks at the both of us in disappointment and tells me to have a seat next to my friend.

As I walked to my desk in the middle of

the classroom I notice some of the girls scowling at me while others offer me a smile and slightly wave at me as I pass by. I was officially the new girl who talked trash to someone I don't know.

Cynthia gives me a huge smile and passes me a note.

To: Sarah

From: Cynthia

Thanks. He's always picking on me and I hate his guts.

BFF - Cynthia

I smile and look over my shoulder at the boy who was staring at me with death ray vision.

'Great Sarah, way to make enemies,' I thought to myself.

Chapter 3:   Meeting Devin

Outside of my first period exchange my day was going great.   I guess it's because Cynthia is in my first two periods and is above and beyond to make me comfortable on my first day.

'I'm so hungry,' I think as I continue to look up at the clock and count the minutes until lunch. I missed lunch this morning because I was so nervous. And my grandma got up to cook me everything I like but I hid out until it was time for me to catch the bus. Man, I am regretting that decision.

"Rrrrrriiiiiiiiiiinnnnnnnggggggggg," I watch everyone scatter towards the door then to their lockers and I quickly gather up my things, throw them in my locker and rush to the cafeteria. I try to slow and wait for Cynthia because I don't want to sit alone but she already has a place for me in line and hurries me to join her.

"Sarah," she says, "You have to get in here

quick because the eighth graders are always horrible."

"What do you mean?" I ask.

"Well, they come in the cafeteria like the own the place and they try to make us go to the back of line when they come in, so you have to get in so you don't get the nasty cold leftovers," she smiles and quickly turns, counting our position in line.

"We're good," she breathes a sigh of relief. "Usely if you get close to the teacher on duty you won't lose your spot. But it depends on the teacher," she says as she rolls her eyes.

I laugh at her and she turns back to me

with the biggest smile.   I'm glad that I have her to be my friend.

Suddenly I hear one of the kids from my third period class mumble, "I don't know what gives them the idea that they are more important than the rest of us," and when I turn around again they were standing at least 10 students back and these taller, louder and like Cynthia said selfish boys and some girls were there.

Leaning into me, Cynthia whispers, "When we become eight graders, we are going to show the under classmen what patience and leadership really is."

With a roaring rumble in my stomach and silence in my voice, I nod my head and agree, "I'm glad you made it to the line first so we can eat and not starve to death like the other kids."

We both laugh and keep our eyes on the prize to being closer to the lunch ladies than our other classmates.

Cynthia slightly turns, "At least we beat the football players in here."

I can't help myself and I turn back and catch the eye of one of the eighth grade boys. He immediately notices me and bumps his friend.

"Ah, that's a new girl... say new girl,

what's your name?" he blurts out.

I try my best to ignore him by turning around and looking at Cynthia like a lost child. She smiles and whispers, "That's Devin the most popular guy here."

I want to faint because he notices me on my first day while I'm trying to keep my position in the lunch line. I try to peek again to see if he was still behind me but I got more than what I bargained for, he was standing right under me and tapping me on the shoulder.

"Eh, maybe you didn't hear me. I said what's your name new girl," he grins and revealing the dimples in his light brown skin.

My eyes wash over his face and I notice everything in the brief moments that I stare at him. He has hazel brown eyes and curly hair. I've only seen hair like that from the boys who were mixed with Mexican and Black back home. He is truly dreamy and I can't remember my name.

Cynthia coming to my aid tells him my name and they both exchange mean looks at each other but never say a word.

He smiles at me and then turns back to his friends in the line and they laugh and mock me being unable to talk.

I hear one of the boys say, "You did it

again, left a girl unable to talk... man Devin you a mac."

They all laugh at my expense and I feel so embarrassed. I see Cynthia immediately getting upset so I tell her, "You know I've always hated eating in front of the boys, especially eighth grade boys."

She agrees and we start talking about the rest of our day. As we make it to the front of the line, our facial expressions begin to show our immediate disappointment realizing that we're going to be eating what appears to be Sloppy Joe.

"Why on earth are they still fixing these

tasteless sloppy sandwiches," Cynthia asks, as if she could do a better job than our school cooks.

All I could think about was the fact that I am too hungry to complain and any lunch that's free is alright for me. I guess because Cynthia's parents pay $1.25 for her to eat lunch she feels that she deserves better. I, on the other hand, understand the importance of being grateful for the little things such as free lunch because $1.25 for lunch means homemade peanut butter and jelly sandwiches for at least four days a school week until my mom gets a job.

It's been hard for us because my mom

worked at a large bank in San Francisco and I guess with my father's income we were okay and could afford lunch. I remember bringing cash to school there to get whatever I wanted so it felt a little weird not having money to buy what I wanted and definitely not to have choices like I did back home.

I smile at Cynthia's rants and think to myself that she's lucky to have two parents that live in the same house. We find a table in the corner where Cynthia was used to sitting from her days as a sixth grader and begin to eat. I look up and here comes my cousin Frank and the eighth grade boy from the lunch line, Devin.

Out of all the available seats in the cafeteria, they choose to sit directly beside us. I knew it was a plan of theirs, because their smiles were entirely too large. I start to get very uncomfortable because Devin made me forget my name. I immediately got shy again and started to pray that he didn't ask me my name again.

As they are eating, Cynthia and I sit absolutely frozen, not wanting to take a chance on picking up our sloppy Joe and spilling it all over our clothes. But we are so hungry so we slowly start to pick at our food.

"Why aren't you eating Sarah," Frank

chuckles to himself as if he didn't already know the answer.

"Oh, I'm not hungry and this meal is certainly not one of my favorites," I respond while trying to be serious.

"Cynthia, what's your excuse," Devin asks flashing his dimples.

"I'm still full from breakfast this morning," she responds.

Cynthia and I attempt to have a conversation with Frank and Devin but they are more focused on their food and ours too. Soon my nerves get the best of me and I am ready to leave.

"Alright guys, we'll catch you later," she says as we leave the table and watch them completely devour our lunch.

I say to Cynthia, "Girl, my grandma would kill me if she knew I missed lunch too."

"I know that's right, so would my mama," she responds.

We both look back one more time at the boys eating all of our food and we hear our stomachs growling. We laugh and say, "Boys," in unison as we head outside for the remainder of our lunch. The only thing I hate about middle school is that the recess areas are all separated so I am not able to get another glance at Devin.

Being outside in Arkansas is weird because it's so hot in the August. I am used to cooler temperatures and activities. At my new school we all just stand around and talk about each other and what we did over the summer as if there are a lot of choices.

Cynthia is so excited that I am her out of town friend that she drags me around showing me off like I am prize. I don't mind because it gives me a chance to make new friends. So I smile at everyone she introduces me to. As we're mingling with the other kids outside, Cynthia and I are separately laughing about what took place in the cafeteria.

"Cynthia, we can't fall off the bandwagon like that anymore," I say as I'm wiping the tears from my face from laughing so hard.

Her response, "I know girl but your cousin is so handsome."

"Gross," I say and make the ugliest face I could.

She laughs and tells me she thinks Devin is ugly.

"Cynthia, you only think he's ugly because he's your cousin," a girl says standing behind us.

Cynthia turns and looks at the girl and responds, "And, I know he's my cousin and he's ugly." She turns her head back around and I stare at her as if I didn't know her.

"He's your cousin?" I ask.

"Yes, I told you that last summer, remember?" she says blowing off my lack of knowledge about the cutest guy I had ever seen. "I told you I had a cousin who was an absolute jerk and that's him, Devin."

Trying to recall the conversation, I decided to just keep our previous conversation going, "Cynthia, since when has a breakfast satisfied you for more than two hours?" I ask knowing that we both are heavy eaters and currently starving like Marvin.

"You know your cousin makes me nervous and besides that would have been tragic if that sloppy Joe ended up in my lap. Don't you think?" Cynthia responds.

I picked at my sandwich and then snuck me a few French Fries before we left. I hope they didn't see me stuffing my face.

We enjoy the rest of our lunch break and I manage to make some new friends who are just as outgoing as Cynthia. I realize that despite leaving my friends in San Francisco that I was enjoying my new life in Arkansas with new friends and a lot more family.

Chapter 4:   A Super-Star is Reborn

I have always been an athlete.   My dad made sure that I was involved in everything he liked.   I am positive that if I were a boy he would have made me play football but he only won with basketball.   My mom made me do girlie sports like cheerleading and gymnastics and it pained both me and my dad.

I woke up excited because today was tryouts for our basketball team. We weren't considered the best in our town but we were definitely better than most schools we played, especially our boys' team.

I went down to the kitchen and my mom was talking to my dad and I could hear them kinda arguing. I was used to it by now. It was probably dad asking mom to come home and her saying no. I honestly still want to go home to see my dad and my friends.

My grandma saw me standing in the kitchen door and told me to have a seat so I could eat breakfast. I love my grandma's breakfast; she makes sure I am full just in case I don't like what they serve at the school. I immediately scarf down my eggs, grits and bacon before I ask my mom for the phone to talk to my dad. She looks exhausted but manages to smile at me as she passes me the phone.

"Hey dad," I say with excitement.

"Hey baby girl. Today is tryouts. You ready to show them your skills?" he asks. You can hear his excitement.

"Yes, sir I am," I say smiling just as hard.

"Good. Remember what I told you about tryouts?" he asks in a more serious tone.

"Play like I am already on the team," I respond as I see Cynthia coming towards the back door with her loud pink book bag.

"Dad, Cynthia's here. Love you," I rush off the phone not even hearing him say it back. I am excited about today.

I meet Cynthia at the door, "Are you going to try out for the basketball team after school today," I ask.

"Girl you know I can't shoot a ball to save my live," she says as she waves to my mom and grandma.

"You surely can shout from the top of your lungs," I say with laughter.

Cynthia has this beautiful voice that everyone loves and adores. Whenever she sings, it makes my heart smile. Before I moved to Arkansas, I would ask her to sing a song and she would sing without hesitation. I know without a doubt that Cynthia's voice will be her ticket to Hollywood in the future.

"Okay, well make sure you're going to be there to cheer me on," I tell her as we start walking towards school.

"You don't need luck, you got skills," she smiles.

The bell rings for fourth period, which is

P.E. for me.

"I'll talk to you later Cynthia," I shout as I'm speeding down the hallway to my locker before heading to the gym.

Since its basketball season, the P.E. teacher, which is the basketball coach, let's the eighth grade players practice on their basketball drills on half of the court. We play volleyball or racquetball on the other half.

I'm playing basketball with the other girls, minding my own business, when Kim, one of the eighth grade players, comes up to me. She picks her ball up from the floor and looks me up and down.

"I hope you don't think you gon' run this team lil' girl," she says.

I just look at her and turn back around towards my classmates.   Kim and I have never exchanged words so I am not sure why she even said anything to me.

I walk over to Clara and ask her, "What's her problem?"

"Don't worry about her, she just mad because she heard you can play basketball. Probably better than her," she says and walks away.

Knowing that I am good, I shrug my shoulders and ask, "So what? Who told her that anyways?"

"Your cousin Frank has been bragging to the eighth graders about your skills.   He's been saying things like, 'There's no girl at Mayfield that can compete with my cousin Sarah, who's trying out for the team.   In fact, if you eighth graders ain't careful, she might come in and take one of y'alls starting positions,'" she says trying to mimic Frank.

I look over my shoulder and instantly realize that Frank was bragging on me but hurting me and giving me more enemies than I needed. 'Ugh, as hard as it is to fit in, I can't believe Frank did me like that," I said to myself.

"I'm Katie by the way," she says as she extends her hand.

"I know what's it's like to be an outsider as well. This is my first year here at Mayfield Middle School too."

I am excited because I finally get to meet someone who understands being the new kid. My spirit is calmed.

"Great, this is my first year too, and I surely miss my friends back home."

"Where are you from?" Katie asks.

"I'm from San Francisco. Home of the San Francisco 49ers or as my grandma would put it, home of the famous Irish coffee," I smile.

"Where did you come from?"

"I'm from Detroit, Michigan. Home of the Lions and automobile capitol of the world," she says with a smile.

"Wow! Why did you come here... to Arkansas?" I said with a frown.

"My dad retired from the military, and decided he wanted to move back south to be closer to our family. So, here we are," she says as she waves her hand around like Vanna White. "What brings you here?"

Immediate sadness overwhelms as I answer, "Divorce."

Seeing that the subject was emotional

Katie says, "I'm sure that's gotta be hard.   But good luck with tryouts today."

"Thanks Katie," I reply as I quickly hurry off the court to grab the tears that were escaping my eyes.   I didn't want anyone asking me what was wrong.   I really miss my daddy, but I didn't want the rest of the world in my family's business, so I went to the locker room to quickly get my emotions together.

Basketball tryouts went well for Katie and I and a few more seventh graders.   The negative energy, from the eighth grade girls, whom my cousin made dislike me, worked to my advantage.   Now, they not only hated the fact that I made the team, but they hated it even more that the coach replaced the starting power forward with me. I was officially on the starting line-up with the eighth grade varsity team.

Unlike San Francisco where there are thousands of kids who play all kinds of sports, being at this school made us seventh graders learn to work with the eighth graders in all things, especially sports. Being on the team means being hated by all of the eighth graders, regardless of how good I am. Thank God I always hear my grandma's voice telling me, 'Those people that hate you are jealous of you.'

So whenever those lam, jealous girls roll their eyes at me, I smile in their face, because it confirms that I have something of value.

Chapter 5:   The Big Challenge

I love having Katie as my friend, on and off the court.   In fact, she's my partner during basketball practice in almost every drill we work on.   Whenever Katie and I practice, the coach seems to point out all of our failures, more   than   the   other   players.   And   it's becoming annoying to the both of us.

Every time we think we have practiced hard, coach says, "I wanna see better."

We don't understand why she puts so much focus on us and we complain to each other all the time.

"Man, coach is getting on my nerves," I say to Katie.

"Yeah, me too. Nothing we do seems right," she says. "Must be how these country folks think. Always trying to keep each other down,"

Katie was known for speaking her mind when it came to matters of Black people not getting along. She had traveled the world with her dad being in the military so she knew firsthand about how other races got along. I on the other hand was used to living and going to school with Whites and Asians and a few Blacks so the issue of race was unfamiliar to me. But I let her rant on about Blacks not being able to get along. It was actually amusing to me to see her so passionate about the subject.

"You know what we should do Sarah?" Katie says with a smile on her face. "We should ask Coach why she's always picking on us."

I agree but deep down inside I am

nervous because the one thing my parents and my grandmother told me never to do is disrespect or challenge adults, especially my teachers.

We plan to stay after practice, pretending to work on our so-called "weakness" so we can ask Coach what her problem is with us.   All the girls clear the gym and we run into Coach Rogers' office, where she is going over notes and plays for our first game of the season.

Standing in the doorway waiting for one another to speak, she looks up and asks, "Is there something I can help you ladies with?"

"Umm, actually there is," I respond while

shoving Katie on the shoulder signaling that it was now her time to speak.

Darting her eyes at me, Katie turns to Coach Rogers and mutters, "Coach, we just want to know the reason why you're so hard on us."

I back Katie up with, "Yea Coach, every time we do something good, your response is it can be done better."

Coach smiles and says, "You girls must have really been thinking about this long and hard for you to come in here and ask me that. So it's only fair to you girls that I give you the answer to your questions."

"The reason I constantly point out your

weaknesses or what could be perfected is because you girls have much potential. When I look at the both of you, I see myself when I was kid. You both love the game of basketball. Now if I don't say anything to you, then you become concerned," she smiles and looks at both of us intently.

We are relieved that she doesn't hate us but that she wants us to be better. Katie and I look at each other and smile and then back at the Coach. We realize that she sincerely wants us to be the best we can be.

"Thanks Coach for being so open with us and sorry for disturbing you," I say with a great big smile on my face.

"Wait, that isn't it," Coach says. "I see the way those boys are getting your attention when they walk through the gym."

"Huh," I say not knowing that she was even aware.

"Huh nothing," I need you two to stay focused, because this team needs you.

"Yes ma'am," Katie and I respond with our heads hung down as if we were caught with our hands stuck in the cookie jar.

"Half of this team don't even like me," I mumble as we're leaving Coach's office.

The last school bell rings and I go to my locker. I am happy that Coach is taking time to care about my skills but I am bummed that so many of my team members don't like me. I meet up with Cynthia along with other students and we walk towards the busses. Normally I walk home from school because I live only a few minutes away, but today wasn't one of those days.

On game days I make every effort to preserve as much energy as possible. I normally eat, take a nap and then head back to the gym to prepare for the big game. It's my routine since I lived in San Francisco.

On days when my mom has to work the evening shift, she gives me permission to ride my bike back to the gym but only if the sun is still out. Being that my mom is single now, she sometimes volunteers to work longer hours for extra money. As a result, she comes home later than usual and almost never takes me to school events.

With this being my first basketball game of the season I feel neglected because my mom is still at work and my dad is in California. Although he did call me before I left the house to go back to the gym I can't help but to feel sad because we're playing a rival school. This is my very first basketball game, and neither of my parents will be in the stands cheering for me.

I'm not trying to be a brat, my mom did come to one of my scrimmage games before the season started, but I want her to be in the crowd today, screaming my name. Maybe I should pray for her a husband, so that she doesn't have to work so hard. Or maybe I should pray for dad to come back into her life, instead of sending us child support.

And if either of them found out that I wasn't doing my homework, they would make me get off the team. It's hard for me to focus on homework, especially when we have a game.

I almost never do my homework at home because of the short amount of time I spend there. Don't mention trying to do it during the boys' game. Man, I wish I could focus on it during the boys' games.

At least I've learned one thing about my ability to focus and do my homework during the scrimmages … it's going to be difficult. The only thing I can focus on is the way Devin flows up and down the court. His skills blow my mind, so much so, I wish I could jump on the court in his path and let him to trip over me. I'd never wash my clothes, maybe even my body from his sweat touching me. Nah, it's not that serious, I'll just take his sweat living in my clothes.

Chapter 6: Game Time

I always love game time because before every game we prepare ourselves with a little music to get our adrenaline pumping and then we pray for protection and the strength to endure until the end.   We know that this game is going to be the game of that will make or break everything because this game is a competitive fight against our opponents.

After our prayer, we do a little dragon chant, then off to the court we go. Before I leave the locker room I say an additional prayer that God keeps everyone safe from injuries because sport injuries are the worst injuries to recover from.

As we run around the court, one behind the other, the crowd roars as if we've already won. I have to admit, my favorite part about the beginning of a game is the introduction of the starting line-up. We rock from side to side and my heart races every time as I wait for my name to be called.

Then I excitement takes over as I hear, the

commentator say loudly into the microphone, "Starting at forward number 23, Sarah Taylor."

Running onto center court, with my purple and gold uniform, the cheers from the fans amplifies. People from all over our school district fill the gym to capacity leaving no available seats. All I can think of is wow this feeling is amazing!

Since we're playing our rivalry school Calvary Lady Tigers, we really have to have our game faces on. This game has been talked about for several weeks now and I'm ready. Our pep rallies are far beyond the usual and we contribute a lot of school spirit. That's why we can't let this team beat us in our own gym.

Three, two, one, the referee toss up the ball and the game begins. The Lady Tigers win the toss-up because their jumper is very tall and extremely larger than ours. She's so tall that we often joke and say she looks like a granddaddy long-leg spider.

"Get back on defense," is all I hear being shouted from the sideline.

Our transition into position isn't quick enough so they immediately score a basket.

Coach Rogers tries to hold it together as she shakes her head and shouts, "Come on ladies, let's make something happen."

When we get down to our end of the court, we setup a play.

Trina, who is our point guard shouts, "14!"

We instantly get into position. Katie notices Kim is open and in shooting distance so she quickly passes the ball.

'Nice pass to Kim,' I think as the ball goes in the basket.

Kim ties us with the Lady Tigers. Setting up for a full court defense, the pressure is back on the Lady Tigers. As they attempt to inbound the ball, our defense quickly steals the ball away. Already on our end, we rotate the ball quickly which keeps their defense from setting up. I notice an opening along the baseline and go to it.

After reaching a point where I feel comfortable, I shout, "Pass the ball, pass the ball!"

I turn to the goal and release the ball towards the net. Swoosh! The crowd shouts as the ball goes directly through the net. I see the entire home crowd jumping up out of their seats.

"Clinching, sounds like money," I shout to my opponents because I love to talk noise during a game.

Shooting a three pointer in a girl's game is like a slam dunk in a boy's game. The Lady Tigers are quick on their feet so we never get side tracked with celebrating. The thing I admire most about the Lady Tigers is their ability to follow up with something spectacular. Every time we score the basket, they do the same thing.

"Get back on defense," shouts a parent from the sideline.

I see right away that this game is going to be an intense battle. They have several outstanding shooting guards who can shoot your lights out, figuratively speaking.

As the last seven minutes of the first half approaches, the Lady Tigers coach changes up the level of intensity. His strategy is to place all of his fastest, race horse, guards in to pressure us. It's times like this that we wished that we hadn't slacked before the season.

All I could think at how Coach was simply trying to prepare us for something like this. While we were training for the upcoming season, some of the other girls and I thought it was cool to walk through our conditioning whenever Coach wasn't around. We seriously took some of our training for granted and now we were faced with the reality of why we needed to be serious.

The Lady Tigers inbound the ball on their end of the court and score the last bucket at the buzzer, taking us into half time with a score of 32-25.

As we head into the locker room, Katie and I run to find each other so we can briefly talk about how horribly we are playing in the first half.

Katie looks at me and says, "Girl they some race horses out there. I don't know what they did to prepare for us, but they are definitely bringing the heat."

All I can do is sigh. The only thing that

bothers me is what Coach is about to say in this locker room. Coach Rogers and our assistance Coach T. storm in while we are all sitting on the benches. We are all quiet to avoid being singled out.

Coach throws her clipboard across the room and screams, "You girls are playing like a bunch of amateurs out there. If I didn't know any better I would think you girls didn't care if we won this game or not."

She continues her rampage, "Trina, you've got to move your feet on defense. You have three fouls in the first half because you're playing defense with your hands. Kim, what's the problem with rebounding? My five year old can get more rebounds than you out there tonight!"

I sniggle as I look at Kim. I'm glad coach called her out, because she gets on my nerves.

"We practice our blocking out drills every single day," she yells and she picks up her clipboard.

Then she looks at our assistant coach and says, "I know what it is, you girls are afraid of a little challenge."

Coach T responds, "I think they're afraid of the Lady Tigers because their first half performance definitely showed it."

Surprisingly Coach Rogers doesn't start kicking the lockers or abusing it with a chair. Instead she gives us new instructions and left the locker room. With a minute left before we have to head back to the court, our captain decides to encourage us with a pep talk.

Karen says, "Ladies, I know this is a real aggressive game and you girls are trying very hard to stay in this ball game. All I have to say is let's go out there and show them what the Lady Dragons are really about. Let's show coach and our fans that we have heart and determination."

With our hearts and minds filled with

motivation, we hustle back onto the court for a quick warm-up before the second half.

At the sound of the buzzer, the starting line-up gets into position, while the rest of the team takes their seats on the sideline. Again the roars from the crowd signify that our fans are truly with us until the end. As soon as the Lady Dragons stretches the floor it causes the Lady Tigers to play each of our players one on one. This set up always works out to our advantage. We all think we're WNBA ready anyways.

Taking back control of the ball game we score back to back points. The Lady Tigers begin to panic and start to make careless mistakes and get in foul trouble.

"Pick your face up off the floor," I say to my opponent, who's really a friend of mine.

The game is going well for me, until I see Devin sitting in the bleachers, eating nachos, surrounded by a group of skinny blonde head girls. I see one girl lean over and whisper in his ear. I try to focus on the game but it's harder than I imagine. All I'm thinking about is 'Who she is and what is she whispering in my future boyfriend's ear?'

Jealousy fills my heart and before I know it I'm dribbling down the sideline. My attention is nowhere on the game. I make myself stumble which allows me to become unbalanced. As I fall to the floor I throw the ball into the bleacher towards the girl who is hogging Devin's attention. The ball goes forcefully underneath her cup and causes her soda to flip in her face and up her nostrils. She had no clue that was coming. Next time she'll focus on the game and not my future boyfriend. I pretend to apologize and continue to play the game.

Although we are in foul trouble, Coach puts in three of her second seed girls to finish off the game. With five minutes left in the game, the Lady Tigers are trailing us. Now is our moment to really step up and shine. I have to come with it because I know that my uncle has gambled on our game. I am playing even harder because I am upset about Devin entertaining those girls.

Katie and I take over the ball game, making the girls from the Lady Tiger to our way. Fortunately, we understand each other like the back of our hands.

Without being told, I already know her next move. Coach puts in some of the smallest girls' which makes it hard to defend our team. Within the last final minute of the game we are leading the game with a score of 65-60.   Coach calls for a time out so we can set up for one more play.   Looking at the clip board, I realize that the last play is for me to complete.   My heart freezes but I look smile confidently at Coach as if I know without a shadow of a doubt that I can do this.

As we get into position, the referee passes the ball to our in bounder, I silently say a quick prayer, "Lord please be with me, but please forgive me first."

Patting the ball the in bounder shouts, "Break!"

The ball goes directly to Trina, while Kim

and Katie set a screen for me to be open at the top of the key. I catch the ball then quickly release it with four seconds to go. Three, two, one the ball hits the rim and then dances around as if it's trying to decide which direction to take. As the buzzer goes off, the ball finally drops through the net, carrying us to victory over the Lady Tigers.

This is a major win for us because the Lady Tigers are undefeated this season. Everyone is celebrating in the gym because this is a great win for us. We don't want to celebrate too soon because we still have to show respect by shaking the other teams' hand.

As we walk to the locker room we shout, scream and jump up and down celebrating our victory.

Coach is surprised at how well we fought back in this ball game. Usually we don't celebrate any more than a few minutes in the locker room after a win, but this time Coach decides to treat us.

"It's Saturday night, so I'll be taking the entire team out for pizza and a movie," she shouts while leaving the locker room.

Cracking the door back open she adds, "Oh, we have to take the short bus again."

It's the funniest thing in the world because we think the little bus makes us look like nerds.   Whenever we ride the short nerdy bus and see our peers staring at us we simply slide down and tuck our heads below the window panes of the bus.   Coach thinks it's cute that we are ashamed of the little bus, so she decides to embarrass us.

We are too excited to care about getting on the bus but once reality sets in and we are at the movie theater we hide our faces and run into the movie theater as Coach T yells, "Let's go Lady Dragons!"

Chapter 7:   Sudden Death

We celebrated our extraordinary win against the Lady Tigers but I had to face reality on this dreadful Monday morning. Ugh, the start of a new week is always the hardest to get adjusted to, especially since I am able to sleep in a lot longer on weekends. When my alarm clock rings, I simply ignore it by pressing my pillow over my head.

My strategy works up until my mother storms into my comfort zone and yells, "All right it's 6:00!"

I use to laugh when she told me how grandma would wake her up at the crack of dawn but it's no longer funny as she is repeating history with me.

Kicking my feet I mumble to myself, "I am not getting up this early when I become an adult."

I roll out of bed and bump my big toe on the corner of the bed rail. You could have purchased me for a penny because I know my mom is close by to hear if I'm up. I stutter walk into to the restroom to get ready for school.

Within 30 minutes of dragging myself out of bed and getting dressed for school, I head outside to meet up with the neighborhood kids. On the corner of my block is where we stand and wait for the bus to arrive. I always wait until I see the bus coming before I cut to the front so I can get a seat. I look to the back of the bus where the high school students sit because that's where the most comfortable seats are. We love sitting back there because it makes the ride to school more exciting, especially when we go over large bumps in the road.

When we arrive to school the bus driver drops us off at the cafeteria. No need to walk around when I can get front door service, right? I don't know why I love eating in the cafeteria in the morning when my grandma loves cooking me breakfast. She's even asked me the same thing but I love being with my friends and rushing to first period before the bell rings. I smile as I enter into the cafeteria because I smell pancakes and sausage.

"Yes," is all I could say as I rush through the line so I could enjoy my pancakes and warm syrup.

At this point I am not concerned about who I sit next to, I just want to eat, so I quickly sit beside this guy who everyone picks on at the school. Everyone calls him, 'Nerdy Boy' and 'Four Eyes,' but to me he doesn't fit those names. Although he does wear his pants rather high and his glasses a kinda thick and do hang off his nose but it's still hard to judge him.

He smiles the biggest smile at me, leans over and asks, "Are you ready to get your report card today?"

I look at him as if he said something wrong and I respond back, "No."

He pushes his glasses up and wipes the dripping syrup from his lips and says excitingly, "These are the moments I look forward to."

Thinking about what my grades are I simply give him a silent response. I couldn't stop thinking about how terribly I've been slacking this past semester. I immediately lose my appetite, so I get up and leave the cafeteria because I knew my mom would kill me.

The bell rings for first period as I am leaving the cafeteria so I rush to my locker to grab my books for my first two classes. I make every attempt to avoid engaging in any conversation because I did not want talk about report cards or anything related to grades again.

"Hi Mr. Jones, how are you today," I say forcing a smile.

Mr. Jones, our janitor, smiles and replies, "Hey baby girl, how those grades looking?"

Typically I laugh when he says something because his voice sounds funny but him asking about my grades makes me even more depressed, "Oh, they're looking good," I answer.

I anxiously bite my fingernails as I take my seat. Mrs. Smith is waiting on everyone to sit down before she passes out our report cards.

Seeing how nervous I am a classmate

beside me leans over and asks, "Is everything ok?"

Knowing that I am disturbed but couldn't blow my cover, I turn to her and say, "I'm fine, thanks for asking."

Mrs. Smith gives everyone a good morning greeting then on to roll call. After roll call, Mrs. Smith decides to jump right into the lesson for the day. Since this week we are learning about the different poets from the past, Mrs. Smith allows us to watch a quick film on Shakespeare.

Immediately, my body begins to relax with the idea that report cards won't be given out today.   So I go back to being social.

My friend Stacy and I write letters to each other since we aren't allowed to talk during class.

Stacy writes, "Shakespeare is very romantic but this film is making me sleepy.   I knew I shouldn't have stayed up all night talking on the phone."

I try to hold in my giggles and write back, "You're right about that."   As we're passing the letter back and forth Mrs. Smith catches us. She is so quick as she takes our letter from us and reads it.

"Stacy and Sarah, I need to see you two

after class," she says with disappointment.

Knowing we are in trouble all we can say is, "Yes ma'am."

It literally feels as if we have been caught sneaking our hands in the cookie jar. I try my hardest to focus back on the film but I am nervous because I don't know what to expect after class. And it doesn't help that Mrs. Smith opens up her large orange folder and takes out our report cards. My heart begins to pound out of control, so loud that a set of drums can't compete with it. I look around at the expression on the other kids' faces and I can instantly tell who did well and who didn't.

"Thank you Jesus," is what I hear coming from the far back corner of the classroom.

Mrs. Smith takes her seat and Stacy and I realize that we haven't received our report cards like everyone else.

'This can't be good,' I think to myself as my stomach curls up into tiny little knots.

The bell rings and everyone leaves for their next class, while Stacy and I stay behind.

"Right here ladies," Mrs. Smith says as she points to the two seats near her desk.

With no one talking in the room, I could hear my shoes squeak as I make my way to the hot seat. Our report cards are there waiting for us.   I hesitate to look down but Mrs. Smith insists that we took a look.

"One by one each of you tell me your grade in English," she says with a disappointing tone of voice.

I hope that Stacy goes first but she looks at me and shakes her head. I swallow my saliva and clear my throat, "D, Mrs. Smith."

Then Stacy follows with the same response.

Mrs. Smith nods her head and say, "Girls, you know I don't like failing my students, but I will definitely do so." She continues, "I don't know what the problem is, but you ladies aren't putting in any effort in this class." She pauses, waiting on us to explain ourselves, "Do you ladies have something to say?"

We both shake our head in unison because we know there isn't anything we can say to make up for our bad grade in her class.

Before she dismisses us, she stops and says, "Oh, the both of you have after school detention today as well."

As we are leaving the class I say to Stacy, "Coach T is not going to be happy when she finds out I have detention today."

We talk about our grades and what our parents are going to do as we head to the office to get an excuse for being late to our next class.

"See you at lunch time," I say to Stacy as we go our separate ways.

As fourth period starts, I dread entering the gym. I really feel like pretending to be sick so that Coach won't bother me today. On days when report cards are given we usually have a free day. The girls who make good grades are able to lounge around and play games.

Meanwhile, the girls who make anything less than a C get disciplined for not maintaining a high standard of excellence in the classroom. Coach looks at our report cards and calls all of us by name.

"For the names that I didn't call enjoy your day, while everyone else report to the baseline," she says.

I knew I would be among the names she didn't call so I had to take my place at the baseline for performing poorly.

"Having to run sprints the entire class period is going to make me definitely pay more attention in class," I mumble to myself as I'm finishing up with my last lap.

I am so ready for school to be out but then I remember that I have an after school detention. 'Ugh. This day can't get any longer,' I think to myself. I slowly walk to my locker to get my backpack and jacket as the last bell of the day rings. It pains me to see some of my walking buddies calling out to me but I'm even more embarrassed that I have to tell them I have detention.

Of course they want to know the details, but I will not be spreading my business to those listening to us yell at each other from a distance so I hold my hand up to my ear like a phone and we all wave bye.

As I enter the detention room I scan the room to see if I know anyone. Sadly to say, I only see some eight grade bullies who I think only attend school just to pick on people.

Either that or their parents send them to school for a few hours for peace at home. I rush for the first available seat right in the front of the classroom as I hold onto my belongings.

"Lord please do not let these people pick on me," I silently pray as I'm watching the time tick away slowly like water dripping from a facet that hasn't been turned off.

When I see Stacy walk through the door, a sense of comfort takes over me. I lean over with a smile on my face and whisper, "Hi."

She places her pointer finger to her lips hushing me up because she is clearly afraid to get caught by another teacher. I agree and pull out my report card to take matters into my own hands. I don't know which was worse, being in detention or my mom's reaction for having a bad grade. Not that my mom is as strict as Stacy's mom or any of my other friends' moms but I just don't want to take any chances. Without a second thought, I sign my mom's name where her signature is needed.

Seeing what I'm doing Stacy leans in and whispers, "What are you doing?"

I whisper, "I signed my mom's name."

With fear in her eyes she leans over, touches my arm and says, "Look, I know you are afraid, but you can get in big trouble if the school finds out that you forged your mom's signature."

She leans back into place as fast as a monkey has time to swing from one branch to the next.

She look around to see if the teacher is watching us, then leans back over and asks, "What if your mom asks to see your report card when you get home?"

I smack my lips, twirl my neck, roll my eyes and whisper, "Relax, my mom doesn't keep up with everything like your mom does," because I know my mom is be too busy to ask for my report cards.

She throws a pencil at my arm and she says, "Whatever bighead."

She and I both know that her mom pays attention to every single detail. In fact, Stacy may be on punishment for the rest of the school year when her mom checks her report card. I remember last six weeks when Stacy made a C in math class; her mom surprised her by doing something very unthinkable. Stacy's mom pulled her off the cheerleading squad until her grade improved. For several months Stacy wasn't allowed to hang out with any of her friends, nor could she talk on the phone. She even had to attend counseling sessions with the schools counselor two days a week for the entire six weeks.

After sitting in detention for an hour, the teacher decides to dismiss us.

"Today has been the longest day ever," I say to Stacy as we're headed to the front of the building to wait on our rides.

I usually walk home after school but the sun has gone down so I ask Stacy if her mom can give me a ride since my mom is working the evening shift. When Stacy's mom pulls up, we both notice the angry look on her face. She makes me nervous so I am not going to ask for a ride home. Instead, I tell Stacy that I'm going to walk.

"Why," she asks, as if she doesn't see that mean, angry tiger look on her mom's face.

"I need to exercise a little bit," I shout with my back already turned as she's gets in the car.

Chapter 8: The Longest Walk Home

Halfway down the road, the thought of me walking alone begin to set in.   Every person that I see minding their own business now seems like they are watching me.   Every sound from the smallest cricket, to the birds in the sky amplifies as I put one foot in front of the other on my journey home.   This truly feels like the longest walk I've ever taken in my life.

Mother knows best starts playing in my

mind as I look and see a group of men coming my way. I start to slow down to see if they were going to go in a different direction. I feel a panic attack coming over me. My heart starts to race faster than a horse in an obstacle course. Sweat pours from every available pore on my body. I am soaked from head to toe.

Just when they are three feet away from me, my uncle Peter pulls up in his white Cadillac and rescues me.

He lets his window down and shouts, "Get in this car!"

I don't even pay attention to the tone of his voice. I just quickly run, open the back door and hop in.

"What are you doing walking by yourself?" he says as he looks at me through the rear view mirror.

I have nothing to say so I shrug my shoulders and look away. As we turn into my drive way, I see my mom's vehicle parked. My eyes almost pop out of their sockets and I start thinking there is no way I will get out of this mess.

"Good, your mom is home," my uncle says while putting the car in park.

Out of all days, why does he choose today to get out of the car? Usually when he sees my mom outside in the yard or on the porch, he blows his horn at her and keeps going. When I ask why he doesn't stop, his excuse is that he's too busy at the moment. My mom says she knows the reason but it doesn't bother her one bit but I know it does since Uncle Peter is my mother's youngest brother and sibling. He sits in the car silently. I can tell he is trying to build up the courage to speak to my mom up close and directly. He realizes that I am waiting on him to walk me to the door so he takes a deep breath and gets out of the car.

With a big smile on my face, I place my right arm behind his back and say, "Mommy is going to be really happy to see you today."

He shakes his head from side to side and barely utters, "I don't know Sarah, I don't know."

I can tell by the tone of his voice that he is unsure of what to expect when she sees him. As I stick my key into the keyhole and turn the lock nothing happens. Mom has locked both latches so I can't get without her having to open it for me. I know at this point that mom is upset with me not being home on time. Even though it's still early, she does not accept me coming home any time after the street lights came on.

My uncle stands at the door puzzled and asks, "Well, are you going to ring the doorbell?"

I whisper jokingly to him, "Yea, after you wipe that scary look off your face."

Within five seconds of me ringing the doorbell my mom shouts, "Who is it?"

She asks as if she didn't already peep through the living room curtains before she walked to the door.

"It's ME mom," I shout with chills all over my body because I know I am about to get in big trouble.

She forcefully swings the door open and she screams, "Get your behind in this house!"

Popping me on the shoulder she screams again, "Where have you been?"

My uncle knows I am in big trouble but he comes to my rescue and interrupts her, "She was with me today. I saw her walking home from school and I picked her up."

He looks at me with a nod telling me to go along with him and continues, "She wasn't ready to come home, so I took her to the barbershop with me to get my hair cut."

My mom can kill both of us with the daggers in her eyes as she asks me, "Is that right Sarah?"

She knows that if I stare long enough into

her eyes that I won't lie to her but this was a matter of life and death so I quickly agree with my uncle. I tilt my head to the side and give the biggest and best puppy dog eyes I can because I wanted to see my friends again.

"I'm sorry I didn't get your permission first," I say with a whimper from the hit she gave me.

I know that my mom and uncle aren't on the best terms right now so I decide to play on her guilt card. Being the super snooper that I am I have listened to countless conversations of my mom on the phone with her best friend crying about missing my uncle, so that is my way out of my current situation. She opens the door wider and tells both of us to come in.

My uncle is frozen and asks, "Are you sure?"

My mom is touched by his uncertainty and reaches out to hug him, "Yes, I'm sure Peter," she says softly.

I know their moment of embrace is my opportunity for escape, so I make a getaway for the stairs, dropping my backpack on the floor and shouting my thank yous to my uncle as I flee to my room. My mission, to get out of my mom's sight so that she won't detect the lies we just told her. When I make it to my room I pretend to close the door but I sneak back out to the top of the stairs to eavesdrop on their conversation. This is truly a moment that my mother needed.

"Have a seat," my mom tells my uncle as she turns on more lights in the living room.

My uncle is uncomfortable so he sits on the edge of the recliner located near the door. My mom sits on the couch that's five feet away from him, so she can have a good view of him. For about 20 seconds, the room is filled with an awkward silence. All I hear is my uncle tapping his feet and my mom clearing her throat excessively.

Eventually my mom coughs to break the silence and quickly says, "I'm sorry Peter"

"Can you speak a little louder, I didn't hear you?" he says poking at her as he always did.

She knows it so she raises her voice and says it again, "I'm sorry Peter."

With a smile in his voice he says, "It's cool big sis."

Happy that the awkwardness is out the room, my mom says, "It's good to see you smile again."

They both laugh at each other like two little kids that made up with one another.

"Now that we are behaving like civilized adults again, can I call and check on you sometimes," my uncle asks.

I hear my mom say, "Sure, in fact I'm having a barbeque this weekend, and you should come over."

Before I could hear him agree his voice gets real low and I do my best to listen but the phone rings and I run in my room to answer it before my mom does.

"Hello," I whisper as I pick up the phone.

"Hey girl, it's me," says Cynthia with a puzzled voice.

"Hey, my mom and my uncle Peter just

made up. I'll call you back, okay?" I say hurriedly trying to catch the rest of the conversation between my mom and uncle.

"Ooooo, you have to fill me in okay?" Cynthia says in amusement.

I don't know if I should be upset that she finds amusement in my family's pain or happy that I have someone to talk to.

"Okay," I say and hang up the phone.

I try to tiptoe back to my position but my mom and uncle are at the door and I dare not chance getting caught so I close the door to my room and place my ear against the door.

The door closes and I hear my mom say,

"Thank you Jesus for bringing my brother back."

My grandmother always says that everything happens for a reason. I smile and turn off the light to my room to see if I can tiptoe out of my room to listen to any phone calls she might make. When I make it to my perch I see my mother pick up my backpack off the floor.

'This isn't good,' I think to myself as she sticks her hand inside the unzipped compartment and moves some things around.

Eureka! She pulls out my hidden and unspoken of report card. I am secretly trying to creep back into my room but her laser focused eyes spot me in the darkness.

"Get yourself down here right now Sarah! I know you're not in your room!" she shouts.

My heart must have abandoned me along with my stomach because I am numb. It's weird how grown-ups know what their kids are doing, without ever being told.

"Yes ma'am," I softly respond, while trying to present a sleepy look on my face.

"When were you going to show me this mess of a report card," she asks while focusing her attention on my D in English.

"What's going on with you up there at your school," she asks with her arms folded and all her weight shifted to one leg?

Not really knowing what to say, I simply shrug my shoulders.

She taps her feet to my lack of response and says, "You can forget about playing in your next two basketball games."

As she prepares to sign my report card she notices that her signature is already there, "Oh you want to forge my signature? Well then, don't worry about playing in the next FOUR basketball games."

I can die right now and I start to cry uncontrollably. I can't believe that my mom won't allow me to play for an entire month, that's not fair. I storm up the stairway, and I could hear my mom say.

"You better walk softer than that before I come up there and give you something to cry about."

I am terrified of my mom when she gets mad because I know she is good on keeping her promises so I lighten my steps and make sure not to slam my door.

As I go into my room I could hear my mom fussing about my grades and the forged signature and I'm reminded of how I laughed at Stacy when her mom took her off of the cheerleading squad. I am so upset that I plop down on my bed and cry into my pillow.

Eventually I realize that my punishment could have been way worse, especially with the fair coming up.   At least my punishment will be over by the time I get to go on my first date with Devin.

Chapter 9:   The Big Question

After a long four weeks of not being able

to practice or participate in our basketball

games, I was thrilled at the thought of after

school practice today.   My new mindset is that

I am going to do whatever I have to do to make

excellent grades this new six weeks so that I

won't have to sit out again.

Going into English class, I immediately ask Mrs. Smith if I could sit at the front, instead of my assigned seat. No one likes to sit in the front of class because Mrs. Smith is more likely to call on them to read more or be a likely participant during discussion time. I am more than willing to take that risk because I don't want to get behind in class again.

Stacy sees that I moved to the front and decides to make her way to the pencil sharpener, where my new seat is located. Carrying a load of pencils, she intentionally drops them near my feet, signaling me to bend down and help her pick them up.   Getting out of my seat to help her, we both bend down and chat.

"Did Mrs. Smith move you?" Stacy asks with a curious look on her face.

"Yeah, she put me here for the rest of the school year," I lie because I don't want to tell her I moved because she is such a distraction during class.

Looking around to see who's sitting near her she whispers, "Now who am I going to talk to during class?"

At this point, I'm thinking, 'Haven't you learned your lesson yet?'

Standing behind Stacy, Mrs. Smith startles us by saying, "Stacy let's get moving, if you're not in your seat when I call roll, then you are considered absent."

Trying not to get in trouble for being innocent, I immediately say, "I'm just helping her pick her pencils up Mrs. Smith."

I'm avoiding taking any chances of having detention again. While getting back in my seat, the eighth grade class president comes on the intercom with the schools upcoming announcements. Everyone in the class, even Stacy, listens and waits for what's about to be said.

"I hope you all are ready for the Columbian County Fair this week. It's going to be a fun filled event that will keep you on your feet. Student tickets are now on sale for five dollars. Remember, early release is Friday, so get your tickets today," he says with excitement.

We all cheer as he closes with, "Let's have an exemplary day, my fellow classmates of Mayfield Middle School."

Everyone is so excited about the annual County Fair. I'm a little confused about the Fair but excited all at the same because of everyone else's excitement. We don't have fairs in San Francisco but nonetheless I'm sure it's something to enjoy. I start to daydream about what going to the Fair would be like. Eventually, I am surprised by my classmate calling my name repeatedly.

"Ugh, what is it?" I snap as I look at her with an upset look on my face.

"Girl Mrs. Stacy calling ya name for roll call," she says as she rolls her eyes at me.

"It's not ya it's your, how did you even make it this far?" I say under my breath

"Sarah's here I shout," hoping she doesn't put me down as absent in her roll book.

I try my best to jump back into my fantasy, where I left off but it was impossible thanks to the daydream snatcher sitting next to me. I slump down in my seat, with my arms stiffly folded, and roll my eyes at the girl next to me. Thinking about my behavior, I drop my head and mutter to myself, "I am being so silly right now." I focus on class and actually enjoy learning for the first time.

I barely make it through my second and third period classes because I can't wait for lunch. I quickly throw my belongings into my locker and rush to the cafeteria before the 8th graders arrive. Entering the cafeteria, I see Cynthia waiting on me in our usual spot. 'She is such a great friend,' I think to myself as I greet her.   For whatever reason, her teacher dismisses them five minutes before the bell rings for lunch.   He tells them that he does this to give them enough time to get in the cafeteria before the crowd rushes in all at once.   You'd think it's because he cares for them, but Cynthia tells me all the time that Mr. Nichols' stomach starts to growls every day at the same exact time, 10 minutes before the lunch bell rings.   I don't know how true the story is, but he is definitely a tall, 350 pound man, who loves to eat.

'Mmmm' I think to myself as a smell pepperoni pizza.   I try to contain my drooling but I can't help but to think of the hot, delicious taste, melting in mouth.   As Cynthia and I move closer to the front of the line, we began searching our pockets and purses for a $1.00 to buy an extra slice of pizza.   After getting our food, we quickly sit at an open table with a group of Cynthia's friends to avoid having available seats for any guys to sit near or next to us.   The last time Frank and his friend, Devin, sat near us was a complete disaster because we were both two nervous wrecks.

"There is no way that I'm going to give away this good meal," I say to Cynthia as we prepare to bless our meals.

"I know that's right" she responds as she's putting her hands together to pray.

Without any further talking, we tear into our meals like two hungry stray dogs. Within minutes, everything from the pizza, to the fruit cocktails, milk and roll was gone. We quickly cover the results with a napkin, relax and start talking about the upcoming Fair.

Cynthia looks at me with a grin on her face and asks, "So who are you asking to the fair with you?"

"What do you mean who am I asking?" I look at Cynthia with a puzzled look on my face.

"Oh that's right," Cynthia says

remembering I am not a local. "Well for the Fair, the girls usually ask the boys out." She grins again, "So who are you asking?"

Trying to hide the obvious answer of the only person I would even consider going with, I act like I am deep in thought and respond, "I don't know yet."

Wondering who her lucky guy is, I ask the same question. She pauses and stares towards the door, "Girl I want to go with him."

"Who is him?" I ask before realizing that her eyes are fixed on Frank and Devin entering the cafeteria.

I swallow hard and respond, "Oh, him."

I try to control my heart from beating out of my chest because whenever Devin is close around me it seems as if my entire body freaks out.

"Sarah, do you want to know what I am thinking?" she asks with a suspicious look on her face.

Afraid to ask what, I begin to question her.

We watch as Frank and Devin take their seats across the room and suddenly she says, "You know I would love to go to the Fair with your cousin and I just know you wanna go with Devin right? So let's ask them out. It'll be like a double date."

This is the boldest thing I've ever considered doing in my life but I can't help but say with confidence, "Okay, come on."

Cynthia grabs me by the arm so hard that she pulls me back down in my seat, "Umm, I-I-I-I was hoping you could ask for the both of us," she says stuttering.

Looking at the way she is biting her fingernails, I know she is really nervous.

"Whatttt, Cynthia seriously?" I shout.

I sit there in disappointment and explain to Cynthia that the only reason I agreed is because I thought we were doing it together.

"I'm nervous too," I tell her as we both are amused at each other.

"Got it, I have an idea," she says excitedly.

"Well, what is it?" I ask looking at the clock and figuring out how much time we have left in the cafeteria.

Pulling out a church program from her purse, she rips it and starts to write in small print, 'Would you and Devin like to go to the county fair with Cynthia and me?   Let me know ASAP?'

She puts the message in my hand and says, "When you go over there to speak to your cousin, slip this in his hand.   And make sure he reads it."

Cynthia is known for coming up with brilliant ideas, but relies on me to complete them.

"Okay," I say to Cynthia in a sluggish tone. This requires me to get closer to Devin, so I'm cool with it.

"You're the best friend ever," she shouts as she's dumping our trash.

Devin's face lights up as he sees me walking towards them. I suddenly have this gut feeling that he likes me just as much as I like him.

As I make it to the table, Devin

immediately stands up and smiles, "Hey Sarah, how are you?"

So glad that he now calls me by name instead of 'Eh new girl,' I quickly respond, "I'm fine."

Frank notices that we are stuck staring at each other so he taps me on the shoulder, "Snap out of it," he says as he reaches over to give me a hug.

I jump and remember the reason I walked over to their table in the first place.

"My bad, hey cousin.   I came over to see how you were doing, and to give you this," I say as I hand him the small piece of paper.

"Pastor who?" Frank asks while reading the wrong side of the torn church program Cynthia decided to write her message on.

"Wait, wait, that's the wrong message!" I flip the torn paper over for him and he begins to read it out loud.

Before he could get past the word "Would," I stop him by placing my hand over his mouth.   Devin is completely tuned in to every word that Frank says.

With embarrassment, I lean close to Frank's ear and whisper, "Wait until I walk away to read it and don't read it out loud."

"Oh, I understand cousin, here give

Cynthia my number and I'll read it in just a second," he says as he hurriedly tear a piece a paper from his notebook and writes his number on the paper.

"Okay, bye guys," I say as I quickly rush out of the cafeteria.

Two seconds out the door, a voice from behind shouts, "Hey Sarah, stop!"

I turn around to see who this loud person is and my heart explodes like fireworks as I realize Devin is trying to stop me.

Before I could get a word out of my dry mouth, he says, "Yes, I will go to the fair with you."

'Dear God, I hope this isn't a dream,' I think to myself as I try to make sure what I'm experiencing isn't one of my crazy daydreams.

I say to Devin, "Can you say that again?"

"Ok, yes I will go to the fair with you?" he says with that million dollar smile.

"Really?" I stand in front of him staring at him.

"Yes, really," he says with laughter.

"Ok," is all I can get out.

He grabs my hand, writes his number in my palm and says, "I'm glad you asked."

As the bell rings for our fourth period class Devin says, "Call me after school."

I try my hardest to keep cool as I walk away from him but what I really want to do is jump up and down shouting as if I just won a million dollar prize. At my locker, I sniff the ink on my hand, take out my notebook and quickly write Devin's number down in my notebook because my hands are super sweaty.

While the other girls and I are stretching before we do our usual warm-up jog around the court, I find Katie and start giggling. Getting her attention, I flash my hand in front of her and start to run fast around the court. She could tell I was up to something, but didn't know what so she chases after me until she catches up.

"Whose number is that? Is that a cheat sheet? What is it?" she whispers.

When we finish jogging the coach separates us into our normal groups, the basketball players in one group and the other girls in another. Boy it felt good to be back in my normal group. When my mom put me on punishment, I was forced to be in the group with the non-basketball players and the basketball players who hated me, enjoyed watching me suffer.

"Welcome back Sarah," coach says as she's assigning different drills for us to work on.

Katie's assignment is to work on free

throws, while my focus is to work on spot shooting.

'Dang, why did she have to separate us,' I think in disappointment.

With us being separated, I'm not able to tell Katie whose number I have on my palm. She has to suffer and wait until practice ends. We rush to the locker room when Coach Rogers blows her whistle and get ready for the next class, all in 10 minutes.

Katie is not a patient person so she hovers over me in the locker room.

"Now, can you tell me what you were flashing in your hand?" she asks.

Opening up my palm, I realize that my heavy sweating has washed away Devin's number.

"Well, it was Devin's number," I whisper with a smile on my face.

"Are you serious?" she asks as if I would be making up this all up.   "No way," she says.

I nod yes excitedly.

She asks, "It's not there anymore, so what are you going to do?"

I open my notebook to show my backup and I scream.   Devin is one of the most charming guys here at Mayfield.   For him to be interested in me must mean that I am attractive to him. We realize that everyone else is leaving the locker room and we still haven't taken our showers, so we jump into the showers get dressed and hurry off to fifth period.

"Are you sure you want to talk to him Sarah?" she asks looking at the paper in disbelief.

"Why would you ask that?" I say as my excitement is starting to leave.

"I just heard some things about him having other girlfriends. A lot of other girlfriends," she looks serious but it's hard to gauge Katie sometimes.

"Well it doesn't matter because my cousin Frank would tell me if he was a player. So keep this between us," I whisper as we head in different directions.

When the last bell rings for the day I couldn't wait to meet up with my walking buddies, to walk home from school. My excitement is bubbling over to tell Cynthia everything that happened when she left the cafeteria. I couldn't get to her fast enough.

"Girl, I have something to tell you," I shout with a shortage of breath, from running to meet up with her.

"Okay, but calm down," she replies while

patting me on the back.

Giving me a second to catch my breath, she excitedly asks, "So what happened when I left the cafeteria today? What did he say? What did he think?"

"Now you calm down," I say to her before she explodes into tiny little question marks.

Slowing down to allow the rest of the group to move ahead of us, I tell Cynthia, "There is good news."

I knew I couldn't tell her my good news until she hears hers first and I hand her a piece of paper, she asks, "What's this?"

I know she's about to be surprised so I

insist that she unfolds it. She opens the paper and she sees in large writing Frank's name and phone number with the response, "Yes, I will go to the dance with you. Call me 555-1234." I give her a moment to celebrate her happiness before I tell her what Devin said and did.

"Guess what?" I say.

"What?" she says staring between me and the piece of paper.

"So did Devin." I say with a big piece smile on my face.

We immediately bring attention to ourselves as we jump up and down shouting like two little preschoolers. The whole walk home Cynthia and I talk about the fair on Friday night.

We eventually calm down from our excitement and I ask Cynthia, "I have a question."

"What is it?" Cynthia asks seeing my seriousness.

"Katie told me in P.E. that Devin talks to a lot of girls. Is that true?" I don't want to believe Katie but she is my friend.

"Honestly, I've heard the same things too but I've never seen any proof. So I guess those are girls spreading it who don't like you," she shrugs.

"I guess," I shrug too and ask her, "So, what are you going to wear?"

"I don't know but it has to be cute," she laughs.

Chapter 10:   Colombian County Fair

Once I finish my homework, I call Cynthia.

Cynthia's 3 year old brother, Jacob, answers the phone in his tiny voice, "Hello?"

I smile at his ability to answer the phone properly and ask for Cynthia.   If I didn't ask for Cynthia right away, Jacob would talk to me for a good 15 minutes or sing ABC's until someone rescued my burning ears. Screaming with the phone to his mouth, he calls Cynthia to the phone.

"Hey girl, what's up," Cynthia asks.

"Are you busy?" I respond.

"No, I'm just watching TV," she says sounding bored.

"Well, let's call Devin on 3-way," I suggest. "I know you enjoy listening to other people's conversations."

We both laugh and I hear her running then the door closing to her room. I assume to keep Jacob out. We sit in silence for what seems an eternity as I get up the courage to dial

Devin's number.

As the phone ring, I whisper to Cynthia, "I'm scared."

As we giggle the strong masculine voice says, "Hello."

I am frozen like an ice cube and the masculine voice asks again, "Hello, who this is?"

'Good Lord Devin is country,' I think to myself but his handsomeness makes me forget all about it.

Cynthia clearly knows I am paralyzed with fear so she jumps in to save me, again, "Hello, may I speak to Devin?"

I pull the phone away from my mouth and

take a deep breath. I sigh because I froze on the most important phone call and let out a sigh. While she is talking I prepare myself to take over the conversation with Devin.

The masculine voice instantly responds, "This is me."

I take one more deep breath and softly and frighteningly say, "Hi Devin, this is Sarah."

I cross my fingers, in hopes that he isn't upset that I called he says, "I was hoping you would call me today."

I quickly calm down when I realize that he was expecting my call. I sit up on my bed and concentrate on our conversation, not wanting to keep him on the phone long, I ask him about his plans for the fair.

"Can I pick you up at seven?" he asks.

"I didn't know you drive," I respond.

"Oh no, my dad owns a limo company, so he'll be taking us," he says with a smile in his voice. "You're gonna have a good time with me, I promise."

"I trust you," I say shyly as I think my first date in a limo is more than enough fun for me.

Leaning back onto my bed, I kick my feet in happiness and realize that I have to ask him about what Katie said earlier today. I clear my throat, "Um Devin I have a question."

"What's up?" he says trying to be cool.

"Someone told me today that you talk to a lot of girls, is that true?" I brace myself for his response.

He laughs and responds, "I get that a lot because I am friendly and because my dad owns a limo company but I promise you that you're the only girl I want to date."

I am floored. I've never had a guy like me this much and all I could say is, "Great, well I'll talk to you later then?"

"Alright beautiful, sleep tight," he says as he hangs up the phone.

Almost immediately, as if on cue, my mom

bursts into the room and says, "I'm sure your brother has been trying to call here and you've been holding up both lines."

Hoping that Devin already hung up, I whisper, "Cynthia, call me later."

"Okay," she whispers.

Although my brother can reach my mom on her cell phone, she prefers to talk on her home phone to save her minutes. My big brother is out of the country so he doesn't get to call home much. So whenever he does call, my mom expects every connection to be available for him to reach us. She's always afraid that she'll receive a phone call one day telling that her son has been killed in a war overseas.

Friday night came so quick and I am excited about what my first date is going to be like. This is so different for me but definitely exciting because I am on a date with the cutest, most popular guy in school.

"Mom, can I wear some of your make-up," I ask.

"No Sarah, you're only going to the Fair, you're not getting married," she says as she shakes her head at me.

I don't care if I am just walking outside I want Devin to see how beautiful I could be, so I start begging my mom to apply some of her make-up to my light caramel skin so I can look more like her. Unfortunately, she says make-up will only make me look older.

Ugh, I can't wait to grow up.

The doorbell rings and I start to get nervous because it's time for me to leave with Devin. I quickly do my last minute checks, like playing with my hair and blowing my breath in my mother's face to see if it is fresh or not. When I make it to the door my grandmother is already there dragging him in. Soon my mother joins her and the two starts an attack of epic proportions. It is like an interrogation from a movie or something. I am absolutely embarrassed.

"Hello, you must be Devin," my grandmother says like a little old sweet lady.

"Yes ma'am," he responds and extends his hand for a shake.

"Okay Nanny and momma, bye see you later," I say while grabbing Devin by the arm and rushing out of the door.

"Wait a minute," my mom says as she grabs me by my arm and pulls me back in the door. "Let's be clear about tonight. You are to be home before midnight." I can't remember the rest because I froze in my tracks looking at both my mom and grandmother in terror.

When they finally let us go we went outside and I see a glittery, white stretched limo parked in the driveway.

"This is a bit much for the County Fair, don't you think?" I ask knowing I can't wait to see the inside.

"It's all high class when you're rolling with me," Devin says with a huge grin on his face.

I see now why all the girls at school like him. He's charming, athletic and he rides around town in class. The only thing close to a limo around here is a funeral car.

Devin opens the door and I hear a loud, "SURPRISE!"

I am in shock as I see Cynthia and Frank sitting on the opposite side of the limo as well as some of Devin's other friends.

I rush in to sit next to Cynthia as she asks, "Am I good at keeping secrets or what?"

"First time ever in life," I respond as we both laugh.

On the way to the Fair, Devin introduces me to his friends and their dates. Most of them are unfamiliar faces because they are eight graders. One of the couples happens to be one of the girls from the basketball team, who doesn't like me.   Surprisingly, she accepts me with open arms and treats me kind.   We arrive to the County Fair and I am ready to walk along side of Devin McConnigton.

All attention is on us as we are the only students who arrive in a limo. Everyone else has been dropped off by their parents.

"Come on beautiful," he says as he grabs me by the hand.   My palms start to sweat.

"I hope you ready for some fun?"

'Anything is fun with you,' I think to myself. "Yes, I am," I say with a huge smile.

"What's wrong Sarah?" Devin says as he looks down at me. "Loosen up, you look nervous."

"I'm sorry Devin," I say sheepishly. "But you make me very nervous."

"Well I have a solution for that," he smiles looking down at me. "Come on guys, let's get on the Zipper."

"Oh no," I say as I tug in the opposite direction.

"Yeah, come on Sarah!" everyone says in unison.

"Are you scared?" Devin asks.

"No, I'm not scared," I lie, searching my mind for a good reason. "But we just got here." I am more nervous about throwing up on Devin than getting on the ride.

"Let's start out slow," I say trying to buy time.

"Okay, bumper cars it is," Cynthia says realizing I am not ready to ride a ride like the Zipper.

A couple of bumps on the bumper cars and the nervous feeling I have vanishes.

"Okay, I'm ready to have some real fun now," I say with a grin on my face a mile long.

"Are you ready for the Zipper now scary cat?" Frank asks.

"Yes, I am bighead," I taunt back as I pass by him to Devin's waiting arm.

We laugh and board the Zipper.   Two to a seat, Devin gets in first.   We go up in the air, twirl round and round and the scent of Devin's cologne keeps me calm.   It is a scent that will be in my mind forever.   I close my eyes to enjoy more of his cologne but a quick bum and we are stuck together like paper and glue as we swing swiftly through the air.   I take full advantage of our closeness and put my arms around him so he can hold me close as I scream loudly.   Before I know it the ride slows down and then suddenly it's over.

"Wasn't that the bomb or what?" Devin asks while I am still holding on to him, pretending to be shaken up.

"Incredible!" I say with excitement as I slowly start to release his arm.

"Anyone up for some cotton candy?" Cynthia asks.

"I am," with the biggest smile on my face as I start to pull Cynthia in the direction of the cotton candy vendors. "Come on let's go get some."

"Wait," Devin stops us in our tracks. "You pretty girls stay right here and let the men go get it."

Seeing Devin being a gentleman, Frank asks, "Do y'all want anything else?"

"As a matter of fact, get us a funnel cake," I shout to Frank who is following Devin in almost a chase.

Cynthia taps me on the hand and asks, "Sarah, you don't think we're asking for too much, do you?"

"No they're our dates, they're supposed to buy us things, right?" I say, remembering what my dad and my mom always told me about dating.

She pauses for a moment, then laughs, "Oh yea, absolutely."

We are both laughing until my laugh is suddenly cut short.

"What's wrong Sarah?" Cynthia asks.

"Do you see that girl over there whispering in Devin's ear? Come on!" I say pulling Cynthia with me.

"Where are we going?" Cynthia asks while I am dragging her, unwillingly, in the direction of the boys.

"To get our food," I reply as I storm over to break up whatever poisonous thoughts this ugly girl is planting in Devin's mind.

Poking Devin in the back I ask, "Is everything okay over here?"

Although I am talking to Devin, my eyes are looking directly at the unknown girl who has a case of the whispers.

"We're fine," Franks interrupts nervously.

"Just waiting on your funnel cakes."

"He can answer me Frank, but thanks," I say rudely.

Realizing that I am not leaving Devin's side, the whispering willow looks back at him and says, "I'll talk to you later okay?"

I don't know if he is afraid to say anything back because the only thing he moves is his head with a confirming nod. I start to get nervous and what Katie said to me in the locker room comes rushing back to my memory. I realize at that moment how defensive I am when it comes to girls talking to Devin.

Frank and Cynthia interrupt the mean looks I am giving Devin with our food.

"Okay, now that we have our food, can we please eat and play some games?" Cynthia asks.

"Why are there only two funnel cakes?" I ask rudely. "Are Cynthia and I supposed to share one?"

Frank hands one to me and says, "The idea is for you and Devin to share while Cynthia and I share one." He hands the other funnel cake to Cynthia and looks at me, winking and grinning.

"Oh God," I mumble.

"What you don't want to share with me?" Devin asks as he steps close to me.

"No, I mean ... yes. It's not that..." I am nervous all over again. We have never really practiced eating at the same time because I always try to be done before he comes into the cafeteria.

"This should be interesting," Cynthia whispers to Frank as we sit down. Devin grabs the first piece and tries it to place it in my mouth. I start to shiver but I manage to lean in close to him with my eyes closed to bite the warm, powered, funnel cake piece.

"Ouch," Devin shouts before I could even

begin enjoying the funnel cake on my tongue.

I jump and immediately say, "I'm sorry. I didn't mean to bite you." I feel like crying and dying from embarrassment.

"I'm just kidding," he laughs hard and I lightly push him and join in the laughter.

"Let's ride the Ferris Wheel," Devin insists.

"Sure," everyone agrees in unison.

The ride feels super romantic, especially with the beautiful lights surrounding us.

"Can I ask you a question Sarah?" he says still looking out at the fair.

"Sure," I say barely audible.

Rubbing my hands he asks, "Why are you jealous when it comes to me?"

I don't know what to say.   I have no idea. I don't want him to jump off the Ferris wheel if I answer like a crazy person.

"I'm not jealous," I say twirling my curls.

"Well, you're not now because you have me with you but when other girls are around me it bothers you," he says giving me a confused look.

My head drops and I know from this point on that our date is ruined.

"Say, don't do that," he says as he lifts my head off my chest.   "Pick your head up.   I think it's cute that you like me that much."

"Really?" I smile so big that I am sure he can count all of my teeth.

"Awe, admit it, you like me," he pokes at me, flashing those dimples.

We both burst into laughter.

"Would you like to be my girlfriend, Sarah?" he asks while pushing one of my curls out of my face. "I like how determined you are and I think I need that."

Before I could answer, our fantasy ride comes to an end.

"Think about it," he says as he squeezes my hand. "Now before we leave let's win a few bears."

We walk around looking for the perfect game to play and with the best prizes.

"Step right up and claim your prize," the attendant from the basketball shooting booth shouts. Devin and Frank both run up, give the man their money and begin shooting as if they are at basketball practice.

"Go ahead take your pick," the attendant says sadly for the fifth time.

Cynthia and I walk away with three bears each. Devin notices it's getting late and my curfew is getting close so he suggests we leave the fair so we can ride around town in the limo before we all have to be home.   When we get to the limo, Devin's father is in a deep sleep and Devin hits the glass hard waking him up.

While we are cruising through the town Cynthia, Crystal and I stand up through the sun roof and shout in unison, "I'm the queen of the world!"

I am so captivated by the fresh air and the limo ride that I don't even notice that Cynthia and Crystal are back inside with their dates.   A little embarrassed I start to make my way back inside the limo but Devin pops out to join me. I am mesmerized all over again, and my heart rate beats rapidly despite the cool breeze.

"So did you think about it?" Devin asks as he holds me close to him.

I decide to act as if I am unsure about his question, "Think about what? Did you know your eyes are so far apart? No I haven't."

He laughs and replies, "So you got jokes, okay. Well will you be my girlfriend?"

"Yes, I will be your girlfriend," I say blushing harder than I have every blushed before.

Devin shouts with his hands raised, "I'm the king of the world."

We both laugh and before I know it Devin leans in and sneaks a kiss on my cheek. I smile and let him know it's okay for him to kiss me again and we both close our eyes and slowly lean in to share another kiss. This is my first kiss from a boy and when I open my eyes I see the church clock sowing 11:30. I pull away from Devin and show him the clock and we both drop back into the limo. Devin lets his dad know of my curfew and we hurry to my house.

When we arrive to my house Devin's dad opens the door and Devin walks me to my door. We both wanted to share another kiss but I could see both my mom and grandmother looking out of the window, so we settle on a long hug.

I wave goodnight to everyone as I walk into my house. 'This is truly a night I will always remember,' I think to myself.

Chapter 11: Valentine's Day Disaster

Devin and I have been dating for several months now and I am in love. There's nothing anyone can say to make me change the way I feel about him. Not even my friends, who constantly bash him. The other eighth grade girls look at me crazy when we eat lunch together and even when he walks me to the seventh grade playground.

I think they're all just angry because the hottest guy at Mayfield is with me. While I am sitting in homeroom, Ricky, the eighth grade class president announces over the intercom, "Attention Mayfield Middle School students don't forget to purchase your sweetheart grams this week because Valentine's Day is this Thursday. You wouldn't want your sweetheart to miss out on a special gift because you forgot. They will be on sale all week starting today right after announcements."

As his voice fades out and my heart explodes with excitement, thinking about what special gift Devin purchased for me. After all, this is our very first Valentine's Day together. Everyone in the class begins to dig around in their pockets, purses and backpacks for loose change to purchase a sweetheart gram for their special Valentine.

Candice, one of the seventh grade flunkies, turns around in her seat and asks me sarcastically, "So are you buying a sweetheart gram for your cheating boyfriend?"

Closing my eyes tightly to keep from exploding, I respond, "Yep and I am getting one for you, being that you're the only person in the entire school that no one cares about."

I roll my eyes to make sure she feels every word I spoke to her. I know she has never liked me since Devin and I started dating instead of settling for a loud mouth like her.

The next few days past and I she doesn't make a sound. 'Maybe she learned not to be a smart mouth anymore,' I thought to myself.

At last Valentine's Day is here. I get up early enough time to curl my hair, as if I had a dance to attend, and search for something nice to wear that reflects this beautiful day. The best thing I could find is my blue jeans and my red and white blouse with hearts printed on it. Arriving to the cafeteria I see balloons, teddy bears and girls opening their valentine cards.

'This is going to be a wonderful day,' I think to myself as I head to homeroom before the tardy bell rings. Before class could begin the eighth grade class president started his morning announcements over the intercom, "Good morning Mayfield Middle School and Happy Valentine's Day to you all! Before we begin our Pledge of Alliance, ladies and gentleman please keep your ears tuned to the daily announcements for Mrs. Washington, the schools secretary, will be calling names throughout the day for you who have a gift awaiting to come pick it up from the office.

Please be aware that if you don't pick up your belongings then I myself will take the privilege in re-gifting it to someone else."

The entire classroom erupts into laughter but we are quickly silenced as he says, "Relax everyone it was just a joke." He continues with the Pledge but my thoughts wonder what my first Valentine's Day gift will be.

When the first bell rings, I am saddened because my name isn't called but I did get two sweetheart grams, one from Cynthia and the other from Frank.

'Wow, maybe Devin forgot about me,' I thought to myself.

After second period, I quickly walk down the hall, passing everyone who already had their gifts from their loves. I run into the restroom, avoiding eye contact with everyone because of the tears forming in my eyes.

'This is insane, how immature I am acting right now?' I think to myself as I am staring at my reflecting in the mirror. The restroom door flies open and Trisha, the quietest, shiest girl in school walks in.

"Happy Valentine's Day, Trisha," I say with a smile as I decide that this day will be beautiful whether Devin decided to think about me or not. Grandma always tells me to never let a man control my happiness for true happiness comes from God above.

With a surprised look on her face she whispers in a soft squeaky voice, "Thank you Sarah for acknowledging me. You are the first person to tell me that today. Everyone seems to walk around me as if I am invisible to them so that really means a lot to me."

Her sincerity touches the bottom of my heart and love fills my veins causing me to extend my arms to hug her.

With joy in my heart I say to Trisha, "You are a beautiful and amazing person. Please, whatever you do, continue to be who you are and don't let anyone change that okay?"

She responds softly, "Thanks Sarah."

Before I could exit the restroom she shouts in a whisper, "Enjoy your gift!"

I turn back around to confirm what Trisha said but she already went into a bathroom stall.

Walking to class Tyson asks, "Sarah did you get your gift from the office? What was it? Who got it for you?"

I don't remember hearing my name being called so I play it off because I don't want to look like a fool, "I'm on my way to the office now. I'll tell you later."

The inside of my body explodes and my

legs feel as if I could take off flying towards the office instead of walking. I run to my math class first to get permission to go to the office and the tardy bell catches me.

"Sheesh, that is a close one,' I think to myself while catching my breath in order to ask Ms. Johnson for a hall pass. She gives it to me and I stroll to the office with the biggest smile ever.

I blurt out in excitement, "This day is beginning to get better and better."

I walk into the office and I see my name on a table in front of a gigantic white teddy bear, with a red heart centered on it. Tied around the bear is a beautiful pink balloon that says, 'Happy Valentine's Day' and a box of chocolates next to it.

'Holy Cow,' is all I can think as my eyes light up and my heart pounds rapidly. I quickly grab my things and leave the office.

As I am taking a moment to admire my gifts I hear the same girl from the Count Fair say to Devin's cousin, Kobe, "Tell Devin I said thanks and I will see him later."

She turns, walks pass me and she rolls her eyes as if she wants to enter into a boxing ring with me. I politely smile at her while focusing my attention on the similar gifts in her hands.

She has the exact same things except her teddy bear is brown, her balloon is white and her box of chocolate is slightly smaller.

"Kobe, Kobe," I say as I run down the hall to get him to before he goes back to his class.

"What is it?" he snarls, "I have to get back to class." He is clearly avoiding eye contact with me.

"Since when have you been in a hurry to get to class?" I snarl back seeing that he is clearly hiding something from me. "Where's Devin today? Why haven't I heard from him yet?"

"Calm down," he says with an attitude.

"He came to school but had to leave because he wasn't feeling well today."

"Yea right," I say in anger. "Spill it and don't you lie to me," I stare Kobe right in the eyes. As I stand there waiting for him to tell me the truth, my heart begins to ache at the near thought of what is about to come out of his mouth.

"Spill what?" Kobe says looking around and down the hall where that girl went.

"What was that ugly girl talking about?" I say pointing in her direction.

"Sarah, do you really want to hear the truth?" he looks exhausted and frustrated.

"Yes I do ... now spill it!" I exclaim, almost yelling.

"Man, Devin bought Kanesha those Valentine gifts," he mutters while staring at the floor.

"For what reason?" I ask as if I am too dumb to know the answer to my own question.

"Because he's dating her Sarah, is that what you want me to say?" he throws up his arms.

Tears begin to fill up in my eyes and I respond, "If that's the truth then yes that's what I want to hear."

He sees that I am clearly upset and wraps

his arm around my shoulders and whispers, "I know Devin is my cousin, but you deserve better than player. He has been dating Kanesha along with other girls at school. He has lots of female friends both here and in the high school."

The tears begin to flow like a river but he continues, "Remember when your cousin Morgan was talking about a guy named Stanley that she really loved and had fun with? She would always talk about the things that they did together and the gifts that he would buy her?"

Sniffling and wiping the tears from my eyes, "Yes, I remember."

"Well who do you think Stanley is Sarah?" he says as he stands directly in front of me. I stand there in disbelief.

I want to believe that his cousin is just jealous of him but that seems to be the furthest thing from my mind. How could Devin be cheating on me with every girl at this school and in high school, even my cousin? My entire body goes weak and the grip that I have on my gifts are weakening fast. Eventually I drop the gigantic teddy bear and chocolates as the balloon floats to the ceiling. I fall to my knees and I cry uncontrollably.

I don't know if I am more embarrassed

than hurt because there are times when I was with my cousin and her friends when she discussed her relationship with Stanley. She described the same qualities Devin has but I couldn't see it. Grandma always told me to be careful with handsome, popular boys because they are the hardest ones to keep.

Ugh, she's right about that.

"If he was going to cheat on me, why do it with someone with cousin," I say to Kobe as he helps me up from the floor.

I wipe my eyes and dust my pants off and realize that kids from other classrooms are peeping out of the door windows. Kobe and I both know we have to get back to class before we are reported as skipping class.

"You can have these gifts Kobe, I want nothing to do with them anymore," I say as I turn and head to class leaving him standing in the hallway. I stop and turn quickly and take the chocolates out of his hands. "I may need them to keep me sane today."

When I enter my classroom, everyone turns towards me, including my teacher and you can feel the tension in the air. 'Boy it feels like I am on trial for first degree murder,' I think to myself as I walk to my seat as if I have shackles on my feet.

Mr. Johnson looks at his watch and then the clock next to the chalkboard and asks, "Sarah, is everything okay?"

I know I couldn't tell him the truth so I lie, "Yes sir, sorry I took so long."

He looks at me as if he wants to say more but decides to continue the lesson. I slump in my seat with my shoulders touching the top of my seat. My arms are crossed tightly across my body and I show no signs of interest as to what is going on around me. I swear I hear Mr. Johnson say study for a test but I can care less.

I let out a long sign and say, "If I don't know it, then I'll just do enough to get by."

I feel someone tapping me on the shoulder so I turn to see it's Charlie. He hands me a folder, "This is from Cynthia," he says in a soft whisper.

I look across the room at Cynthia, she points at my eyes and says something with her lips as if I can read her lips effectively. I open the folder and unfold the letter and it reads, 'Sarah, where have you been and what is going on with you?'

I look at her and shake my head signaling nothing is wrong then I continue reading. 'Don't say nothing is wrong because I can tell from the train tracks your mascara left behind on your face. You've either been crying from laughter or something terrible has happen.' Before I write her back I wipe my face with the sleeve of my shirt. And it reads ...

To: Cynthia
From: Sarah
Time: To Eat
Date: Valentine's Day February 14th
Mood: Sad ☹
Message: W/B

Wuz up?? Nothing much just chilling in the cut writing you. N*E*Ways let's cut to the chase. What have you been up to? Today is Valentine's Day and it has been the worst day this entire year. Devin did send me a gift to the office along with a gift to Kanesha Brown (The same exact gifts). You know I'm going to tell you all about it. I am done with Devin as of 20 minutes ago but I'm not worried at all. Lots of nicer boys want to go out with me anyways. I feel so bad, because I stopped talking to Stacy. She was only trying to warn me about Devin before I got hurt. Hey, I got to go but we will talk more after school.
  Best Friends!!!!

HAPPY VALENTINES DAY
Sarah & Cynthia!!

I fold up the letter nice and neat and label it for Cynthia's eyes only. I quickly hand her the letter as the bell rings and I head off to third period.

On my way to class, Clara, the new girl from Tulsa, Oklahoma says, "A teddy bear was in the hallway earlier with your name on it. I take it as if that was your balloon floating around all lonesome as well."

Taking no ownership to my cloned gifts I shrug my shoulders and say, "No, those aren't mines. Maybe someone else has the exact same name as me, how ironic is that?" I say sarcastically.

I rush pass her wondering, 'How does she even know my name?'

School has been out for a half an hour and already Cynthia, Katie and I are on the phone planning a way to get their mom's to bring them over to my house right away. Luckily Cynthia can walk over but she has to have approval of her mom first.

"You better hurry girls, I don't think I can wait any longer," I've gone through my room and gathered up every item Devin has ever bought me, given me and simply things pertaining to him and thrown them into an enormous laundry bin.

"I'll be over as soon as my mom comes out of the restroom," Katie says with impatience in her voice.

"What should I tell my mom?" Cynthia asks knowing that homework and chores has to be done first before she can go anywhere.

"Tell her we need to work on a class project," Katie and I reply in laughter because we both had the same exact lie in mind.

"Quiet guys," Cynthia whispers as she's about to ask her mom for permission.

"Momma, can I go over to Sarah's house real quick? She broke up with her boyfriend today because he cheated on her and now she's really heart broken." I push the buttons on the phone and start blowing in her ear to get her to stop telling her mom my business but we're not surprised when she tells her mom the truth.

What we are surprised about is hearing her mom saying "Oh yea baby, go and be with your friend but hurry home before dark."

We all hang up the phone and I continue my rampage in my room searching for any and everything Devin related. I look out the window and notice Stacy getting out of the car with Katie. I rush to the front door in amazement and disbelief.

"Sorry Katie, I brought Stacy because you two need to make up," Sarah says lowering her eyes.

"Sorry Sarah about your heart break," Katie says as she walks closer to me. I could tell she wants a hug.

"No, I'm sorry Katie for not listening to you." I say reaching out to my friend for a hug. We walk back into my house and upstairs to my room where they see a large pile of clothes, pictures, letters, drawings and even jewelry waiting to be destroyed.

"This is why I need you here. I need for you all to witness the ending of a chapter that was never meant to be," I say as I stare down at the charm bracelet Devin bought me for Christmas last year.

We all sit momentarily in silence until we hear Cynthia running up the stairs. She notices our silence and comes to stand by me hugging me tight. She never says a word. We all carry the things downstairs to the backyard as if we are about to perform some form of a ritual. I grab the gas can next to our lawn mow and sprinkle gas over the pile. I light a match and throw it onto the pile, trying not to burn myself. As I watch the blaze quickly grow, so does my sadness.

I start crying and eventually my knees get weak and I start to fall to the ground. Cynthia, Stacy and Katie hold me close and comfort me on the ground. We all sit together watching the blaze die out as my hope for believing in love slowly dies too.

Valentine's Day for me was supposed to be a day filled with love and happiness but instead it has been replaced with tears, pain and heartbreak that overwhelm us all.

Chapter 12

Hawaiian Spring Dance

At two months has passed since my backyard bond fire. And I have apologized over and over again to Katie for not believing her about the rumors she heard about Devin. Of course, she accepts my apologies and eventually she becomes irritated when I apologize again. So I stop so we don't have another argument.

By now everyone at school has heard about the bonfire but no one has approached me about it until today.

Kristy, one of my classmates, eventually builds up the nerves to ask me, "Sarah is everything ok."

I'm not sure why she even cares so I calmly respond, "Yea I'm fine, why you ask?" I am getting more annoyed by the second thinking one of my best friends told what happened at my house that night.

"Well, I heard your house caught on fire and y'all have nowhere to stay," she says as if she is trying to whisper.

I can't contain myself so I laugh out loud and ask her, "Where did that come from?"

Before I know it another student, who is clearly eavesdropping answers, "Naw, that's not what I heard happened.   I heard you was mad at yo mom and burnt all her clothes up."
By this time I am annoyed and I go into attack mode, "It kills me how country people are from here!"

Obviously Kristy thinks I am responding emotionally from the make believe fire at my house so she asks, "What size does she wear? I'm sure my mom has something she can fit."

Before I can correct the rumors about me being homeless or destroying my mom's clothes, that flunky I had to check earlier in the school years walks by rolling her eyes and says, "You should be ashamed of yourself. And oh, I told you!"

Before I know it I say loudly, "No what you should be ashamed of is coming to school looking like a chicken clucked around in your head."

"What?" she yells and puts her books down. "I bet you want say it to my face?"

"If your face wasn't so monstrous, then I would do it proudly," I respond.

The class bursts into laughter and tune in to see what's next.

"Listen here, Ms. Think She Better Than Everyone Else, I don't know how things work in California, but down here we stick together."

While she's talking, two of her dirty looking friends stand up, shoulder to shoulder with her. I am nervous but I refuse to let it show, especially when my boyfriend sharing cousin Morgan stands up to defend me.

"Oh, it's not going down like that," she says folding her arm and standing beside me.

"Sure isn't," Cynthia shouts as she seemingly comes out of nowhere to stand on the other side of me.

"It's like that Morgan? You don't even respect your cousin since you were dating her boyfriend," the flunky says.

Morgan is as solid as a block of ice and says, "It's like that, now what are you going to do about it?"

Mrs. Smith walks into the room as the bell is ringing and sees us all squared off as if we are on some old western show. "All of you go straight to the office!" she yells.

"Great, now I'm in trouble again," I mumble to Cynthia as we make our way to the office.

"Sarah, wait up" Morgan shouts from behind.

I roll my eyes and I turn to see what she wants.

"What do you want Morgan? You know you didn't have to stand up for me especially since you've already made me look like a fool once. You thought I wouldn't find out about you and Devin?" I say angrily. "Well I did and not from you!"

"Come on Sarah, it's not worth it," Cynthia says as she pulls me away.

"No hold on," I say snatching away from Cynthia. "I'm sick of girls like you who have no respect for other girls, not even their family. No as a matter of fact, you don't even have respect for yourself. You knew you were dating Devin but you lied to me and called him Stanley. How could you?"

"Sarah I'm sorry. I didn't mean to go that far with Devin," she says with tears in her eyes.

"Sorry?" I yell at her. "You're my cousin, you shouldn't have even entertained him in the first place but I guess family doesn't go very far around here!"

Tears start to flow down my face and my heart starts to hurt, "I just wanna go back to

California where my dad is."

I turn to Cynthia hugs me and holds me as we walk to the office to await our punishment. As we are leaving the principal's office the only thing I want to do is sit by myself and not be bothered. Unfortunately, I have to go back to class and look as if I at least care about today's lesson.

'Thank God he only gave us a warning and not detention,' I thought to myself.

Cynthia, seeing that I wasn't in the mood to talk, writes me a letter:

> From To: Sarah
> From: Cynthia
> Mood: Mad
> Message: What's up? Don't let those girls get under your skin. At least no one knows about

what really happen that night.   Anyways, are you still going to the spring dance?   Let me know.

BFF Cynthia and Sarah

Yikes, I forgot all about the dance that's coming up in two weeks.   I don't want to talk about what just happened so I tell Cynthia that I am not sure if I want to go to the Spring Dance anymore.   I mean after all, I don't have a date and I'll wind up having to watch my ex-boyfriend ride around his new girlfriend in the limo he rode me around.

I'm honestly torn because half of me says no way I am not going to the stupid dance, while the other half wants to see and experience what all the hype is about.   From what I heard about last year, the seventh and eighth grade spring dance off the hook. Last year their theme was Mexico, so the school had a Mexican fiesta dance. I wonder if they served Mexican food too because from what I see around here Black people only eat chicken and collard greens.

Luckily, this year theme's is Hawaiian and since I've been to Hawaii with my mom and dad, I'll know exactly what to wear... if I go. 'Ooh, I can already see the beautiful colors everywhere,' I think silently. Boy if I were at home with my dad again I would ask him to take us to Hawaii right now.

As per our daily routine after third period,

I rush to my locker and then find Cynthia somewhere in the lunch line.

"My bad about earlier Cynthia, I wasn't in the mood to talk," I say with a long face hoping she isn't mad at me.

"No worries friend, I'm just glad you're good," she smiles. "I didn't want to get expelled for beating those trolls down but I would have," Cynthia smiles and gives me a big hug.

"Awe, how sweet?" I say blushing at my friend's sincerity.

"You're my bestie girl," she says.

"You're mines too Cynthia," I say still

smiling from her bear like hugs. "One of the best friends I've ever had."

Breaking the awkward affectionate moment in front of everyone she sees that we're having tacos today and both of our faces light up. We hurry to wash our hands and move through the line like two professional stunt car drivers. Our strategy for skipping in line is to find someone ahead of us and talk our way in. The same strategy works on the lunch ladies when we want some more food.

"Hey Mrs. Harrison, you look really lovely today," I say with the biggest smile ever.

"Awe, you're so sweet," she says as she

drops two scoops of taco meat instead of one.

I smile and thank her for my extra portion and listen closely as Cynthia does the same thing to receive her double portion. We hurry to our seats so we can devour these tacos.

As we're eating Cynthia asks, "Sooo, are you going to the dance or not?"

"Ugh, you would talk about this, right now," as I take another bite of my taco.

"Yea, because we need to take a break from all this school work. I'm tired of working, Cynthia says challenging me with her eyes.

"Just wait until you have to work a nine to five then," I say as we laugh. "But seriously

Cynthia I don't have a boyfriend anymore remember. What do I look like going to my first dance alone?"

Smiling from ear to ear and with a song in her voice she says, "That's not what Frank says."

I perk up because I haven't talked to Frank because I feel as if he betrayed me too by being Devin's friend, "What? What did he tell you?"

"He says Devin wants to ask you to the dance," she says with a grin.

I am immediately confused because I don't know how to feel about what I just heard. Cynthia knows what I have gone through to get

Devin out of my system now she tells me this as if it's nothing.

"Really Cynthia?" I ask.

"Wipe that mean look off your face, I talked with him too," she responds in her motherly tone.

"And...," I say urging her to continue.

"And he feels really bad for hurting you," she says with a serious look. "And I believe him."

"You're only saying that because he's your cousin Cynthia," I say rolling my eyes.

"No he did say that," Cynthia looks sincere but I'm not sure I am ready to believe her.

We all sit in silence even our other friends as we all hear the news of Devin's apology.

"Well, he needs to tell me that," I say as I go back to eating.

"Maybe he'll tell you now," she says as she sees Frank and Devin entering the cafeteria.

I immediately lose my appetite and tell Cynthia let's go.

"But I'm not done with my tacos," she says with lettuce and taco sauce on her mouth.

"I'm not either, but let's go. You know I can't stand to look at him," I say standing up and walking towards the trash can.

Cynthia takes one last bite before she gets

up.   Standing at the trash can thoughts of Devin run through my mind and I have to admit that I miss spending time with him.   Every time I see him, I'm reminded of the good times we shared together.   Devin sees about to leave the cafeteria so he rushes over to catch us.

"I see you didn't eat all of your grapes. What is it with you and not eating all of your food?   You know grapes are good for you," he says awkwardly trying to break the tension.

I don't say anything to him. I just give him a cold empty stare was all I can give him at the moment.

Cynthia breaks the tension and reminds me that

we'll be late for our meeting on the playground.

"We'll talk later Devin," she says as she grabs my arms and pulls me away towards the seventh grade playground.

I pull away gently and tell her I'll catch up and stop to stare at Devin. I could feel the tears forming in my eyes so I take a deep breath.

"Why do you want player? Why did you have to play with me?" I ask through my frustration.

"Sarah I'm sorry. I didn't mean to hurt you. I just got caught up in all the attention I was getting," he says with his eyes locked on me.

"Sorry for what, being the jerk that you are." I say as I turn to walk away.

He pulls me by the arm, "I'm sorry for thinking about myself and not about your feelings.   I've changed, just let me prove it," he says softly.

"Why haven't you apologized until now, if you're so sorry?" I can't move because I miss him being close to me.

"Because I didn't know the right time to tell you," his voice is still low.

"How do you plan on proving yourself now Devin?" I ask while trying to hide the excitement in my face that he is begging me to give him another chance.

"I can start by taking you to the spring dance," he asks as he drops down to one knee.

Everything in me wants to make him beg like a dog but I am too embarrassed at the attention we are getting so I pull him back up and we both laugh.

"Okay, I'll go with you on one condition," I say as I pull him close for a hug.

"What's that?" he asks looking into my eyes.

"Don't ever do this to me again," I say as I close my eyes.

"I've missed you Sarah," he smiles.

"I've missed you too Pooh Bear," I say before I run off to talk to my friends before the recess bell rings.

Friday night is now here and I am excited about what my first spring dance experience is going to be like. I beg my mom, again, to apply some of her make-up to my face, claiming that it will make me look more like her. After I am fully dressed, my mom comes into her room with her small jewelry box and pulls out her beautiful Tiffany's, necklace and bracelet. She places the necklace around my neck and the bracelet around my tiny wrist.

She hands me a pen, with a contract that says, "If you break it, you replace it." I am not sure if she is serious or joking but I hurry up and sign the paper. As I'm spot checking small details about myself, the doorbell rings. Insisting that mom opens the door, I quickly rinse my mouth mouthwash and look up my nose for any surprises and self-checking my breath before I head to the living room. Walking down the stairway, I see Devin standing with a dozen of purple roses waiting on me. I am astounded that he remembers purple is my favorite color. I'm still not buying the idea that he's changed all of a sudden.

Devin approaches me and places the beautiful roses in my hands.

"Smile for the camera princess," mom says.

She looks so happy as she says, "You're beautiful baby."

Leading me out of the house Devin's attempts to impress me continues with the limo we went to the County Fair in parked in the driveway.

"Remember, I ride in class," Devin says as to say I better keep him because it don't get any better than him.

Once again the crew, Cynthia and Frank

are in the limo and we arrive to the dance in style and all attention is on us, again. Devin looks at me and compliments me on how beautiful I am.

Blushing from cheek to cheek, I respond, "You're very handsome as well."

At this moment all the bad memories of what Devin took me through are a blur. 'I hope I don't mess these pictures up,' I think to myself. I can count on one finger how good my pictures come out and before I know it, it's our turn for photos.

"Next in line," the photographer says.

'Okay Sarah.   This should be simple. Just

a basic pose, standing slightly face-to-face with Devin,' I tell myself over and over again. We look at the photographer, smile and the flash is so bright I blink very hard. Just as we are about to walk away, the photographer ask if we can do another pose. I immediately think 'I must have looked horrible the first one that's why he's asking us to do it over.' My heart sinks in my stomach. I can't think of any other pose to do because the only poses I'm use to were with my mom and dad.

Devin sees my confusion so he directs me to bow my head and he kisses me on the forehead. I know these pictures are going to horrible so as we head over to see the pictures I close one eye to brace myself. To my surprise, the two shots are the most beautiful pictures I have ever taken in life. A relief comes over me and I grab Devin by the hand and lead him to the dance floor.

The DJ is doing an excellent job up until he decides to play slow jams. I slowly watch the brave couples stay on the dance floor, as the kids whose mothers gave clear instructions to stay back leave the dance floor.

I so desperately want to be one of the kids who leaves so I ask Devin, "Would like to go get some punch?"

Disappointed in my escape attempts, he reluctantly agrees. Cynthia and Frank exit the dance floor too because I am sure her mother warned her about dancing too close. The DJ must have noticed the massed exodus from the dance floor so he plays a more upbeat song and we all go back to the dance floor.

This night couldn't get any better. We even participate in Hawaiian Limbo contest and other Hawaiian themed activities.

"Girl, do you see those twin sisters over there staring at me?" I ask Cynthia as we wait our turn in line at one of the games.

Cynthia practically begs me not to say

anything to them.

"Well who are they?" I ask looking at her with a confused look on my face.

"Troublemakers," she sighs. "One is an ex-girlfriend of Devin's."

My mouth drops open and all I could say is, "Wow, who hasn't he been with in this town?"

Devin must have a radar for trouble because he sees how the girls are looking at me and how angry I am staring back at them so he suggests we take a ride in the limo around the town and enjoy the night air and maybe get something to eat.

"Why are we leaving so soon, do you have something to tell me?" I ask Devin angrily.

"Naw, it's just that those two girls are crazy," he says nonchalantly.

As we're leaving the dance, one of the twins throws an empty cup at the back of my head and hits me.

She then shouts, "You better leave, cause it was about to get ugly in here."

I can't control my anger anymore. I am so sick and tired of dealing with these crazy Arkansas girls. So I storm back in and walk right up to the twin I thought hit me with the cup and punch her in the face. Almost immediately everyone gathers around us and block the teachers from breaking us up. What I didn't anticipate in my rage is that I am going to have to fight both of them. My rage keeps me on my feet for as long as I could stand and I grab enough hair and hit enough faces to make a lasting impression but it's hard to fight two girls at once so I end up on the ground as they are pulling my hair and ripping at my dress.

Eventually the punches lighten up as I hear, "You don't have anything to do with this." And then I see one of the twin laying on the ground next to me. Cynthia has jumped in my fight to protect me and boy can she fight. She literally knocks both of the girls on their butts while I'm covering my face on the ground. I never knew Cynthia could fight. I get up off the ground and help her, as if she needs my help before Devin and Frank burst through the crowd and pull us so hard that I hear Cynthia's beautiful dress rip.

My mom's Tiffany necklace is destroyed as are our dresses. I am devastated by the way I acted but getting away was more important now. We run quickly out of the building before the chaperon can pinpoint who actually fought. My heart is once again broken because the most beautiful night of my life is a nightmare, all over Devin.   Inside the limo Cynthia refuses to say anything to me and my cousin Frank looks at me as if I'm a monster. He doesn't understand how hard it's been for me being Devin's girlfriend and the attacks I've endured.   I look at the others in our group and they too are avoiding eye contact with me. Finally, I look over at Devin, who is sitting quietly with his hand on his face as if he is thinking he has made the wrong decision to apologize to me.

I can't take the silence from everyone so I stand up to through the roof of the limo to get some fresh air.   Immediately tears start to come down my face as I look out at the moon.

"I want go home," I start crying hysterically.

"My dad is taking you home," Devin says as he makes his way where I am standing.

"Don't touch me Devin, you've brought nothing but trouble into my life since I've been here," I push him away.
Confused he asks, "Sarah, what are you saying?"

"I'm done Devin," I cry. "I just got into a fight over you, so I'm done."

"But I love you, Sarah," he says with tears.

"It's too much drama, Devin... I just want to go home," I say wiping the tears away from my face.

I leave Devin standing outside of the limo and sit back down and bury my face into my hands until I am home.

When I get out of the car, Devin's father looks at me and says, "I told my son longtime ago those games would catch up with him when he meets a girl he really likes."

His words comfort me but I know I now have to face the reality of how my mother is going to take the fight I just had.

Chapter 13: I'm Sorry

Luckily, my mom is angrier at Devin for being a cheater than she is at me when I tell her what happens. She only punishes me about fighting and breaking her necklace so she tells me I'll be spending my Easter Break in the house cleaning and reading. She also tells me that my allowance my dad sends is hers. I don't complain or fuss because I know my punishment should be worse.

I know when I get back to school I'll be the subject of conversation and I know eventually I'll be suspended for my actions so I begin to dread the end of Spring Break before it even starts.

Day in and day out I ask my mom if Cynthia called and every day she tells me the same thing. "No."

I know I can't talk on the phone but I thought at least she would let me talk to my best friend. I am devastated at the thought that I may have lost my best friend because I lost my temper and got into a fight over some girl Devin use to date.

Fortunately, my grandmother is not as strict as my mom. While my mom is at work my grandmother lets me call other friends to check on Cynthia and tells me how many times Devin has called to check on me.

Unfortunately, everyone tells me the same thing… they haven't heard from Cynthia. They all seem irritated with me when I call, even Frank. When I ask them why they are so dry, they just tell me that I shouldn't have responded and gotten Cynthia in trouble with me. They even go as far as to say that they warned me about Devin's playboy ways so I shouldn't have been surprised when another girl gets up that I am with him.

I try to defend myself but they are right. Too many of my friends warned me about Devin but I didn't want to listen. I thought I was the honey, the bee and everything in between. But I was mistaken. I was just another girl to add to his collection. And for that I may have lost my best friend and all of my other friends too.

I know that I definitely lost Devin but I am finally okay with that because I never want to get to a position where I am fighting over any boy or man. And not to mention getting double-teamed and beat up. If Cynthia hadn't jumped in, I am sure I would have been beaten to a bloody pulp.

On Saturday, my mom usually goes in to work overtime at her job and I just can't bear not talking to my best friend anymore so I beg my grandmother to let me walk to her house. She agrees but tells me to get my butt home before my mom does or I'm on my own.   I high tail it to Cynthia's house and bang on the door screaming her name.   Her mother swings the door open angrily and looks at me as if I were a serial killer coming to take Cynthia's life.   She scares me but I am determined to see my best friend.

"What do you want little girl?" he mother says nastily.

"I'm so sorry for what happened at the dance," I say immediately. "I got tired of being picked on by girls at the school because of my boyfriend and I lost my temper. I never asked Cynthia to jump in nor did I think she would." I am pleading with her to understand.

"Why wouldn't you think she would jump in?" she snaps back. "You mean the world to her Sarah."

I start sobbing uncontrollably, "She means the world to me too and I need to see my best friend... please may I talk to her? Just to say hi?"

Her mother doesn't seem to be moved by my tears, so I slowly turn to leave still crying uncontrollably.

"Cynthia, come here now," I hear her mother yell.

Before I could turn around all the way Cynthia is hugging my neck tightly and we're saying how much we mean to each other and apologizing. I thank her mom with a big hug and she warns the both of us to never do anything like that again but tells us how proud she is of us for sticking together.

Cynthia and I sit on the porch for 10

minutes trying to catch up before I tell her I have to leave before my mom gets home. We hug again and I dash off with the biggest grin on my face, waving behind me until I turn the corner.

I make it home literally in enough time to get upstairs and pretend like I've been reading the entire time. My grandmother smiles at my joy and heads back to the kitchen to finish cooking dinner for us. I grab my notebook and start to write Cynthia a letter for every day I've been trapped in the house and unable to speak to her.

I can't wait to get off punishment,

although I think I'm going to be on it for the rest

of my life.

Chapter 14: Another Great Escape

Just as I thought, everyone at school is talking about the big fight at the dance. When Cynthia and I walk into the cafeteria for breakfast, the looks on everyone face, including the cafeteria workers is hard to take in. So much so that we almost skip breakfast altogether but we're too hungry from running out of the house to avoid another lecture from our mother's, so we tough it out.

"Cynthia and Sarah I heard that you two were the ones who beat up the Davis twins. Is that true?" asks a random seventh grade boy.

Neither of us say a word because we vowed to deny everything unless they pull out evidence like a video tape.

"Come on, you can tell me," he keeps egging us on. "I won't say nothing."

Cynthia and I look down at our plates and finish our breakfast before we have to go to first period. I am so nervous because I know Cynthia doesn't like pressure and she hates lying. I finish my breakfast first and jump up indicating to Cynthia to join me and she does.

As we walk out of the cafeteria it seems like every student is in the hallway waiting on us. All we hear as we walk to our lockers are whispers and we see some kids even pointing at us.

"Keep cool Cynthia," I whisper.

"Oh, I am," she says as she lifts her head and strolls to her locker. "Like I said those girls deserved to get what they got because they messed with the wrong girls."

I am amazed at her confidence so I follow suit and lift my head as I walk to my locker behind her. When I open my locker a letter falls out. I flip it over and see that it's from Devin. Cynthia smiles and tells me to open it but I don't want to deal with him or his drama anymore.

She snatches the letter out of my hand and holds onto it and whispers, "I'll keep this until you're ready to hear what he has to say."

She winks at me and reminds me we don't have much time before the bell rings. I'm still amazed at the new confidence my friend has but I like it. We run off to class anticipating that the entire class will be a buzz with questions about the dance.

Immediately after we enter first period,

we're told to go straight to the office. I could hear the oohs from our classmates and my heart sunk. I am going to be on punishment now for the rest of my life. I could feel the tears forming so I look to Cynthia who doesn't seem bothered at all.

'What is going on with her?' I wonder and turn around and start the long walk to the office for our sentencing. In the office the ugly Davis twins are sitting quietly trying to look like victims. Cynthia snarls at them and turns to me and tells me she is ready for round two for tearing up her dress. I tell her it's okay and if I have to work the rest of my life, I'll buy her a new one. We both laugh and the secretary hushes both of us.

In the principal office I see her mother, my mother and the twins' mother as well as Devin, Frank and their parents. Cynthia's tough girl demeanor quickly fades as this is a surprise for the both of us.

It seems like we spent hours in the office with everyone explaining their side of the fight. I confessed to losing my temper and admit that I should have handled it better and Cynthia admits to her part. The twins however, act as if they did nothing wrong and even say they were attacked by us out of the blue. What I didn't know is that those girls have a history of starting fights and Devin's dad has had to threaten them several time to stay away from his son.

Devin can't keep his eyes off of me but I make sure to look away because I don't want any more trouble. The principal agrees that the twins started the entire fight, just based on their prior history of fights with other girls Devin has dated and suspend them for the remainder of the school year. I know that our punishment is going to be worse, but he tells us to go back to class and warns us to not come into his office again.

I'm floored but I hear Cynthia's mother ask the principal if he is coming over for dinner on Sunday and he agrees.

I look at Cynthia and ask her, "Why did your mom ask him that?"

Cynthia laughs, "That's my uncle."

We both laugh as we go to our lockers to get our things for second period.

"My mom talked to him when I came home as did Devin's dad," she says as she walks away from me. "Whatever you did to my cousin, it's worked because he really loves you."

I stand in the middle of the hall watching her walk away.

The rest of the school year is relatively uneventful. Cynthia and I have a reputation for the two girls who beat up the Davis twins and to not be messed with. My grades are awesome and I am enjoying practicing my basketball skills with my friends. Katie, Cynthia, Stacy and I finally get to sleep over each other's house with the promise that we'll be able to do it more often once school lets out.

I thought I would hate being at Mayfield but I guess living here is not so bad. I can't wait for the summer though. And I wonder what's in that letter that Cynthia says she'll let me read when I'm ready?   Who knows but I'm

glad to be here with my friends.

◀▶ SARAH

Made in the USA
Middletown, DE
01 December 2021